Summer Ghost

Seven Seas press and purchase enquiries can be sent to Marketing Manager Lianne Sentar at press@gomanga.com. Information regarding the distribution and purchase of digital editions is available from Digital Manager CK Russell at digital@gomanga.com.

Follow Seven Seas Entertainment online at sevenseasentertainment.com.

TRANSLATION: Evan Ward
COVER DESIGN: H. Qi
INTERIOR LAYOUT & DESIGN: Clay Gardner
COPY EDITOR: Meg van Huygen
PROOFREADER: Dayna Abel
LIGHT NOVEL EDITOR: T. Burke
PREPRESS TECHNICIAN: Melanie Ujimori, Jules Valera
EDITOR-IN-CHIEF: Julie Davis
ASSOCIATE PUBLISHER: Adam Arnold
PUBLISHER: Jason DeAngelis

ISBN: 979-8-88843-191-7
Printed in Canada
First Printing: August 2023
10 9 8 7 6 5 4 3 2 1

Summer Ghost

original story by

loundraw

written by

Otsuichi

translation by

Evan Ward

Seven Seas Entertainment

Table of Contents

One

Summer Ghost

THE SPARKLER BEGAN to glow as I lit the few grains of gunpowder embedded in its tissue-paper tip. Only a few seconds later, this initial spark swelled up into a slag—a molten dewdrop dangling delicately from the end of the crooked stick; a mote of warmth, carved out from the cold. Suspended upside down, this orb of light burned most brightly from the bottom, as the resultant updraft from the tiny pocket of heat it created only drew in more and more oxygen to fuel its flame. And so on it burned in the crisp night air, bright and brittle until at last it saw fit to begin shedding sparks, and a firework was born at last.

For a moment, the crackling embers scattered wildly—each firing off in their own arcs before bursting and branching out in all directions—but then, all at once, the fizzling fountain froze over. The chirping insects in the surrounding fields and forests fell silent, and the flow of time seemed to slow to a crawl. This was a sensation I hadn't felt in over a year—a strange phenomenon that could only be experienced here in this spot where the fabric of our world grew thin, and the fetters that kept us bound to it came undone.

Aoi was standing right beside me, with Ryo directly across from us.

The three of us stood huddled close together in a triangle, as if gathered to marvel at the sparks where they hung frozen in midair.

"Been a long time since we all got together like this," said Aoi.

"Yeah, no kidding," I said with a nod. "I've been so busy lately that I couldn't afford to make the trip back home. Sorry you two had to wait up for me."

"Don't sweat it, dude. We're just glad you could make it," Ryo said, casting his gaze up into the sky. "Man, it's hard to believe it's been a whole year though, huh?"

Far off in the distance, the skies overhead had begun to fade from black into a deep, navy blue. It was that most fragile time of night, just before the first rays of morning light crept up over the horizon, and for a moment, I could almost see her there with us—that pale, fleeting specter I once knew.

Two

Summer Ghost

SUMMER VACATION, one year prior.

I stood on the rooftop of a tall building. As I gazed down on the street below, I wondered how many seconds it might take for my body to hit the ground if I were to hop the railing and jump off, right here and now.

I heard that falling to one's death was the second most common method of suicide in Japan, accounting for about 7 percent of all male suicides—and especially prevalent in urban areas with no shortage of tall buildings to choose from. The only thing you had to be careful about was to not hit anyone else on your way down; there were countless cases of innocent pedestrians being killed by a suicide victim who chose to jump down onto a busy main drag. But given the general correlation between suicide and mental unwellness, chances were that most of these victims were simply not in a state of mind to spare a thought for the people down below.

I wondered what type of building I might choose to commit suicide. Obviously, it'd be ideal to pick something more than twenty meters tall to ensure an instant death upon hitting the ground. *Maybe I should write up a shortlist of candidates when I have some spare time,* I thought idly to myself—but just then, I felt the buzz of my smartphone alerting me that I received a new message. Apparently, the two people I was waiting for had just arrived.

I headed back inside from the rooftop and took the elevator down to the floor with the café we agreed to meet up at. Upon entering the establishment, I was greeted by soft music, cool air conditioning, and two pairs of eyes staring in my direction from a round table near the window. One girl, one boy, both of high school age and dressed in casual attire. I didn't recognize either of them, but I could tell from their glances that they had to be the two I exchanged messages with over the past several days—Harukawa Aoi, and Kobayashi Ryo. I walked over to greet them at their table.

"Aoi-san and Ryo-kun, I take it?"

"Oh, yes! H-hello!" said Aoi, slightly flustered, and she gave a little bow to greet me. She reminded me a bit of a small animal—petite, timid, and cute.

"Nice to meet ya, Tomoya-kun," said Ryo, raising one hand. His street-style fashion sense certainly left a bold impression, but his chiseled features and confident body language were just as striking.

I pulled out the sole unoccupied chair at the table and took a seat. It was a small round table for three, which meant we were all seated 120 degrees apart from one another. First, we ordered drinks. Then, we proceeded to make casual small talk for a while to help shake off some of the initial awkwardness that seemed inherent to these sorts of first-time meetups. It turned out that Ryo and I were both the same age—eighteen-year-old high school seniors—whereas Aoi was one year our junior. We all lived within a few stations of here by train.

After a few minutes, once we broke the ice and a lull in the conversation hit, I felt we were more than ready to delve into the topic at hand. I pulled out the map from my backpack and laid it out across the table.

"All right. Now let's talk about this Summer Ghost, shall we?"

Way out in the suburbs, near the very edge of the prefecture, there was an old, abandoned airfield. Originally constructed at the behest of the Imperial Japanese Army during the Second Sino-Japanese War, it later saw extensive use during the final years of World War II. At that time, it was particularly used as a takeoff point for fighter jets sortied to repel enemy bombers throughout the countless air raids conducted over the Greater Tokyo Metropolitan area. Following the war, it was converted into a small airport to service some of Japan's smaller outlying islands on an irregular basis. However, it ultimately went bankrupt and closed down some years ago. The terminal building and the control tower had already been dismantled, so all that remained now was a large runway in the middle of a wide, open field. Supposedly the prefectural government had been discussing how to better make use of the land for many years now, but it had been left utterly untouched since as far back as I could remember. It was hard to believe it wasn't simply forgotten.

Every so often, you'd hear stories about groups of rambunctious kids or teenagers who would sneak their way onto the fenced-off property, just for the thrill of it. And it was from the stories those groups told of their experiences that, over the past few years, a new urban legend had been born—namely, that of the Summer Ghost.

"Our first reported sighting dates back to three years ago, when some junior high kids on summer vacation trespassed onto the property to light off some fireworks without permission," I explained, using my pointer finger to indicate the abandoned airfield's location on the regional map—an empty, rectangular space in the middle of a rural sector that was otherwise just rivers and open fields. "Then, the following year, a group of elementary schoolers claimed to have encountered a similar apparition. Also in the summer. *Also* while playing with fireworks on the runway, supposedly."

"There's our pattern, I guess..." Ryo mumbled.

"You got it," I said. "It seems it only appears during the summer, and only when fireworks are being lit. Those are the two major constants I found in every eyewitness account—of which there are several more, by the way. Some dad who took his whole family out there, a motorcycle gang that wanted to party, a loner who wanted to see the ghost for themself... All of them spotted it in the summer, and all of them were setting off some kind of fireworks."

"You keep saying 'it,' but it's really a she, right? Assuming the rumors are true, that is," commented Aoi.

"Yeah. A woman around the age of twenty, apparently," I said. I pulled out my sketchbook and a pencil from my backpack to draw a quick visual aid as I explained further. "Long black hair, long dark skirt... Probably somewhere in this ballpark, if I had to guess."

I quickly sketched out the image I'd constructed in my head of the Summer Ghost based on the various bits and pieces of information I could glean from the eyewitness accounts. Once it was done and I lifted my pencil from the page, Aoi looked down at the crude drawing, apparently impressed.

"Wow, Tomoya-kun," she said. "You're a really good artist."

"Yeah, I was in art club back in junior high. Don't draw too much anymore, though."

Pretty much all I drew back then were rough pencil sketches like this—usually portraits from the chest up, largely realistic. It felt a bit strange (and perhaps a bit melancholy) to realize that I was already feeling rather nostalgic for those days.

"So she's a ghost, but she's still got legs, huh?" said Ryo, also examining the sketch.

"According to our primary sources, yeah," I said. "Not that no one's ever gone on the internet and told lies before."

Still, these were the only accounts we had of this seasonal specter—this Summer Ghost. And if we wanted to verify them, then there was only one thing we could do.

"Well, they also said she's the ghost of a woman who committed suicide, right?" said Aoi. "Wonder how true *that* part is."

"Hard to say. Guess we'll just have to ask her when we get there, won't we?"

For that was exactly what we'd gathered here to do—and why we'd gotten in touch with one another in the first place. We needed to see this apparition for ourselves.

After leaving the café, we made a quick stop at a nearby hardware store to buy a wide variety of fireworks. Then, we hopped aboard the bus and set off on our little journey. Not long after pulling away from the station, we left the commercial district behind, and the buildings we could see from the bus windows grew fewer and farther between. This wasteland of suburban sprawl grew sparser and sparser, and the other passengers got off one by one until eventually the three of us were the only ones left aboard.

Finally, as we approached the edge of the prefecture, we disembarked at a bus stop in what could only be described as the middle of nowhere. After double-checking the map to get our bearings, we headed down the unpaved road toward the abandoned airfield. Soon, the sun began to set over the western horizon, and the skies above were gradually dyed a deep red.

All of a sudden, Aoi stopped dead in her tracks.

Ryo looked back at her. "What's up?" he asked.

"Oh, uh... Nothing," she replied. "I guess it's just...finally settling in for me that we might *actually* see a ghost out here. Maybe I'm kinda getting cold feet. I dunno."

"Well, if you wanna head back, go for it. But me? I wanna see this thing."

And with that, Ryo set off walking once more. I followed suit. After a few moments' hesitation, Aoi jogged up from behind to rejoin us. It seemed she couldn't pass up this opportunity either. None of us knew whether the Summer

Ghost was real or not, but it was our mutual desire to find and speak with her that brought us here today.

It wasn't every day you got to ask questions of the dead, after all.

We had questions like... What does dying feel like? Or being dead, for that matter? Did it hurt? Does it still? How excruciating was it?

We all wanted to know exactly what death was like, and no living soul could answer such questions for us—but a wandering spirit who experienced it herself surely could.

As we reached the crest of a grassy knoll, we looked down to see a wide-open plot of land, surrounded on all sides by a chain-link fence. And there in the center of the rectangular lot sat the old, abandoned runway. Even from afar, it was plain to see it had gone unmaintained for many years. Where the airport buildings once stood, there now remained only large concrete foundation slabs. The whole place was overgrown with weeds.

We looked it over and talked among ourselves.

"So that's the airfield, huh?"

"Sure looks like it."

"And how do we get inside?"

"I'm sure we'll find a way. C'mon."

The three of us made our way down the hill. The chain-link fence enclosing the site was warped and rusted, and as we made our way along it, we found a break in it where someone had apparently wrested their way in by force. We crouched down, slipped through the gap, and made a beeline for the runway, parting the tall grass as we went.

"Oh, wow... Just *look* at this place! This is incredible!" Aoi was giddy with excitement.

The vast, open field reached all the way out to the horizon where it brushed up against the sunset sky. Ryo set down our shopping bags and began to lay out our extensive collection of fireworks across the runway. We'd certainly come prepared.

"So you really think this'll work, huh?" he asked.

"Maybe, maybe not," I said. "It could just as easily be nothing more than a rumor—a story some kid on the internet made up for kicks three years ago, which other people then picked up and ran with."

"Why three years ago, specifically?"

"There weren't any recorded sightings before then. You couldn't even find a single mention of the term 'Summer Ghost' prior to the sudden uptick three years ago. It's like the legend just materialized fully formed, right out of thin air."

Ryo placed a large fountain-style firework a short way away on the asphalt. I pulled out a lighter, walked over to it, and lit the fuse. Shortly after, its stocky tube began to emit a shimmering shower of green and pink sparks. It wasn't even fully dark out yet, but the striking colors were still dazzling enough to earn a few *oohs* and *aahs* from Aoi.

As the smoke wafted up into the air, so too did the smell of burnt gunpowder. It was an acrid scent, to be sure—but it wasn't one I personally disliked. It reminded me of being a little kid again, running around the neighborhood and setting off fireworks with my friends.

Then, after about twenty seconds or so, the fountain of light sputtered out its last spark and was extinguished. As quiet fell over the runway once more, we were all left with a strange sense of melancholy dissatisfaction. Like, *"Oh... Was that it?"*

"Here, Ryo-kun! Let's try one of these next!" said Aoi, perking up as she rummaged through one of the shopping bags for another firework. She seemed to be really enjoying all of this now—almost to the point that I wondered if she forgot why we were even lighting off fireworks in the first place, given how spooked she seemed at first.

As the last sliver of sun dipped down below the horizon, the skies finally started growing dark. The sweltering summer heat died down, and a cool breeze began to blow as the stars poked their heads out from behind the clouds. There were no obstructions out here to block our view—just an open plain, twinkling stars overhead, and an array of bright, multicolored fireworks briefly illuminating our faces as we set them off, one by one. We hadn't even prepared a fire bucket or anything to extinguish them in case something went wrong; we were just letting the used ones pile up at our feet. But no matter how many burned-out fireworks we accumulated, no phantom appeared before us.

"Welp, looks like our ghost friend's a no-show. And we've been at this for a *while* now too," said Ryo. "Better head back soon. Don't wanna miss our ride."

He had a point. Considering how long it would take us to hike back to the bus stop, it would probably be smart to pack up and get going right about then. Not that there were really any fireworks left to pack up and take home, mind you—we even went through the entire set of little kiddy handheld fireworks. All that remained now was a pack of traditional Japanese-style sparklers that came bundled with them.

"All right. There are the last ones," I said, handing Aoi and Ryo each a sparkler. They were the semi-crooked kind wrapped in colorful tissue paper, each with a small pinch of gunpowder embedded in the very tip. I lit both of theirs with my lighter before lighting my own.

"Y'know, for a minute there, I actually believed we might see a ghost out here," Ryo confessed. "Feels kinda stupid, now that I actually think about it. But hey, at least I got to come out here and blow some stuff up with you two, right? Was pretty fun, honestly. A better time than I've had in a while. Thanks, guys."

Ryo was not, evidently, the type to let his emotions show outwardly. One probably couldn't tell just from watching him silently gaze at the fireworks all night that he was enjoying himself as much or as loudly as, say, Aoi had been. But from the way he described it now, it sounded like he actually had a really good time.

I was glad to hear that.

There was something to be said for having the ability to enjoy yourself, even when you know you're standing right at death's doorstep.

With the gunpowder in my sparkler now lit, I watched as the familiar red droplet formed slowly at its tip, softly sizzling as it swelled up into a molten marble before it started scattering sparks into the wind. Each orange speck then burst and branched out, like needles from a glowing pine branch, as they shot off in all directions around the sparkler's tip.

"Yeah, I had fun too," said Aoi. "This was the first time in a long, long while that I've been able to just kick back and enjoy myself, without having any intrusive thoughts."

Just then, our sparklers went wild, shooting off even more sparks, and faster than before. The crackling grew louder and louder as they branched and burst into even more elaborate patterns—until eventually they reached a crescendo, accompanied by a flash of blinding white.

"Ouch! That's hot...!" Aoi cried out. She dropped her sparkler as she yanked her hand back, and the sparks immediately subsided.

"What the hell was that?" asked Ryo.

"Don't ask me..." I said. *Maybe we got a pack of faulty ones?*

An eerie silence fell over the area. The wind stopped, and the softly swaying grass grew still. Not even the faint buzzing of insects could be heard anymore. Only our sparklers still burned on—except now, I could see the arc of each solitary spark as they traced slow and gentle curves in the night. The pine-needle patterns that burst and bloomed so erratically before now hung still in the air, as if the very flow of time itself had slowed to a crawl.

"What *is* this...?" Aoi breathed out, bewildered. I followed her line of sight to see exactly what had baffled her—the sparkler she relinquished her grip on just a moment ago was still suspended in midair a few feet off the ground, as if it had been frozen in its freefall.

Something was not right. It was as if we'd been plucked out of the flow of time and dropped into a world at rest. Soon, even the sparklers stopped shimmering, and all I could see were a few microscopic beads of light hanging in the orbit of their molten tips. I quickly recognized that those were the actual sparks, and that the only reason the "sparkling" phenomenon occurred was because time had been moving fast enough for their light to leave a momentary afterimage along the arcs in which they fell.

And then I felt it: There was a presence here, watching us.

But it wasn't just me who noticed it, apparently. Ryo and Aoi raised their heads and started nervously scanning the vicinity as well. A palpable tension loomed around us—as if the very air had suddenly gone cold and stagnant. Unbreathable.

Then, from over my shoulder, I heard a sigh...yet I knew, rationally, there should be no one standing behind me.

Warily, I turned around—and there she was.

A woman now stood at the edge of the cracked runway, right where the overgrown weeds met the pavement, having crept up on us without a sound. She bore a startling resemblance to the impression I'd drawn in my sketchbook at the café prior to our departure. It was a young woman with long, black hair, a deathly pallor, and yes—two stockinged legs slid snugly into black Mary Janes that stuck out from beneath her dark, ankle-length skirt. And yet despite all these vivid details, there was a surreal, almost hallucinatory quality to her. She seemed fleeting, ephemeral—as though if you tried to reach out and touch her, she'd simply vanish into thin air.

Aoi and Ryo were both too stunned to say a word. I was pretty shaken up myself, admittedly, but I felt compelled to at least *try* to say something.

I called out to her. "Summer Ghost... Is that you?"

There was no reason for me to think she'd answer to that name in retrospect, given that it was simply a moniker made up by supernatural enthusiasts on the internet, nor was there any reason to assume we could hold a conversation with her to begin with. But my mind wasn't working properly at the moment, and it was all I could think to do. The ghost, meanwhile, simply tilted her head and stared at us curiously.

It was then that I noticed she'd been standing on her tiptoes this whole time. No—upon closer inspection, the tips of her toes weren't even touching the ground, and instead floating a few centimeters above it. It was as if her entire body was weightless, or at least lighter than air. There could be no doubt about it: We were looking at a true apparition.

The Summer Ghost was *real.*

In certain corners of the internet, there were private message boards where disaffected youths gathered to discuss a variety of socially taboo subjects—suicide being among them. For some, these forums were a sort of coping mechanism—a place where they could go vent their frustrations to people in similar situations, and whom they knew would actually take their suffering seriously. And for others, these functioned as a place to seek advice regarding the most painless or practical methods of taking one's own life.

It was on one of these message boards that Aoi, Ryo, and I first met. I'd started a thread asking if there were any other high schoolers in my area who were contemplating suicide, and the three of us started corresponding from there. After exchanging a number of messages, it became pretty clear that we were indeed all high school students living in the same general area, not just creeps trying to meet up under the veil of anonymity. And, perhaps most importantly, we were all quite serious about committing suicide.

Aoi was being bullied relentlessly at school, and her teachers refused to do a thing about it. According to her, not even her family could be convinced to care about her or her problems even for a minute. It was making her life a living hell.

Ryo was suffering from a serious disease that was all but incurable. According to his doctors, he didn't even have a full year left to live. So, he made up his mind to go out on his own terms—before his illness ate away at him completely, while he still had his dignity.

My problems, meanwhile, seemed pretty darn minor by comparison. I wasn't a victim of bullying, nor was I suffering from some terminal disease. Sure, my life was stressful—but more than anything, I was just...disillusioned with living. There was no major impetus that I could point to—I was just sick and tired of it all and had been for quite a while now. Simple as that, really.

"So are there still, like...high school cliques and stuff after you die?" Aoi asked.

"Y'know, I'm not sure, really. Think we're pretty much on our own for the most part, though."

"Phew. Okay... That's good to know. I'd *rather* be alone, honestly."

"Yeah, I get that. Not always a good time being around other people, is it?"

The Summer Ghost had proven to be far more talkative than I ever would have thought and was fielding questions from Aoi. Now that our initial shock had died down, we were all surprisingly calm about this whole ordeal. You'd think that most people would panic and run for the hills upon seeing a ghost (and indeed, that's exactly what she claimed all of the people who previously encountered her had done). The three of us, however, were not so easily spooked, given that we came here with the express goal of having a conversation with her about death in the first place.

When we explained that to her, she seemed utterly baffled. "You're a weird bunch of kids, you know that?" the ghost had said.

Her real name, incidentally, was Sato Ayane. I could only assume that this had also been her name while she was alive—barring, I suppose, the possibility that she was some nature spirit that had never been human to begin with. In terms of appearance, she did indeed look to be around the age of twenty. In addition to the aforementioned long black hair and long dark skirt, she wore a thin silver necklace with a blood-red pendant around her neck. Her beautiful visage and delicate figure brought to mind the sorts of women that one only ever seemed to see in museums—in paintings displayed behind panes of glass and velvet ropes. There was also a gloomy air of melancholy about her, and a sort of transient paleness to her complexion—both of which only served to accentuate her mystique. As far as I could tell, she could choose to levitate at will. At the moment, her feet were planted firmly on the ground as she crouched down to Aoi's level.

"You seem awfully curious about the world after dying, Aoi-chan," said Ayane.

"Well, yeah. I mean, it's not like there's anything good about *this* one," she said. "School is literally torture, and no one gives a crap about me—I figure I might as well just die and get it over with already."

"I see," Ayane replied. "Well, I'm sorry to disappoint, but I can't be of much help to you there. I don't really know much about the world after death either."

"What do you mean? Aren't you living there right now?"

"Living" in the world after death...? Isn't that a bit of an oxymoron? At the very least, it struck me as an odd choice of words on Aoi's part—and apparently, Ryo felt much the same. I turned to my side and shot him a quizzical glance, and he reciprocated with a shrug of his shoulders. The two of us were standing a short distance away, listening in on the girls' conversation.

"Thing is, I think I'm kind of stuck in limbo," explained Ayane. "I've just been wandering around this general area ever since I died. I've never encountered another ghost either, so I'm guessing the vast majority of people just move straight on to the next life and whatever comes after this."

As she gazed wistfully up into the night sky, Ryo turned to me.

"Hey, so what's the deal with these sparklers?" He was referring, of course, to the three sparklers that were still hanging in the air, a few feet off the ground. Ryo and I had let go of ours shortly after Ayane appeared, and just like Aoi's, they now remained suspended in freefall.

"Pretty sure it's because time's stopped for everything but us," I said.

The tall grass all around was no longer swaying, and I could even spot a few winged insects here and there, frozen in mid-flight.

"Yeah? And how the hell does *that* work, exactly?" he asked.

"Dunno. Could be that we've entered some heightened state of consciousness, where our senses have been sped up to such a degree that it feels like everything's moving in slow motion. So slow that it's not even perceptible."

But even if our minds *were* moving faster, that wouldn't explain why we were still able to move our bodies at normal speed, or why our vision hadn't gone dark due to light entering our retinas at only a fraction of its normal rate. Why weren't our clothes and bodies frozen in place like the grass and the insects? How could we walk around and talk to one another like normal? Perhaps we slipped into some strange liminal space, like a gap between dimensions where the usual laws of physics didn't apply.

"Eh, whatever," Ryo said with a sigh. "No point in speculating about the supernatural, I guess."

Aoi then called out to us from across the runway. "Hey, you two! Come over here and join the conversation!" Apparently, the girls had hit a lull in their chat. "I mean, you guys had stuff you wanted to ask Ayane-san too, didn't you?"

"Nah, I'm good, thanks," said Ryo. "I'm just glad we actually got to meet her. That's more than enough for me."

Aoi leaned over and whispered in Ayane's ear. "Just FYI, Ryo-kun's got some horrible disease," she said. "He doesn't have much longer to live."

"And who gave *you* permission to share that, huh?!" Ryo yelled back—though I could tell from his tone that he wasn't actually all that bothered. If anything, he seemed to be in an awfully pleasant mood ever since the Summer Ghost appeared, like a guy who just received some very good news. I couldn't help but wonder if meeting this ghostly presence had softened his fear of death to some degree. Perhaps the knowledge that there *was* some form of conscious existence after death, like we could see with Ayane here, had invited some much-needed serenity into his soul.

We were, after all, a group of teens who were seriously contemplating suicide. But that in itself did not mean we were unafraid of death, or even more than that, being erased. Completely and utterly ceasing to be. This was the main reason we wanted to see if this supposed ghost was real or not. We wanted to ask her about her experience with death, as one who already went through it, and to glean some insights on how to best end our lives.

But since Ryo claimed he didn't have any questions for her, I raised my hand instead.

"So what are some of the biggest changes you've noticed after dying?" I asked. "As in, things that are different now, compared to when you were alive?"

Ayane looked at me. There was a deep but beautiful darkness in her eyes—every bit as alluringly unknowable as the night.

"Oh, gosh. Where do I even begin?" she said. "Well... I don't have to pay my taxes anymore, for one thing."

"That's not what I meant. Let me clarify," I said. "I'm asking if the world looks or behaves differently for you now that you're dead."

"You're not much fun at parties, are you?" said Ayane, folding her arms with a rather displeased expression on her face.

"Yeah, no kidding," Aoi chimed in, placing her hands on her hips. "You're never gonna get a girlfriend like that, Tomoya-kun."

Apparently, I was being chided for brushing Ayane's joke aside. "My mistake. I apologize."

"You don't *sound* sorry," replied Ayane. "Are you sure you're not just saying that to placate me so we can get back to what *you* want to talk about?"

Now *that* threw me for a bit of a loop. Not that I wasn't already well aware of this little character flaw of mine—I always had a bad habit of trying to gauge what response was desired from me based on the other person's body language, and that strategy had gotten me this far in life, at least—but rarely did I ever *truly* mean the things I said.

"All right, why don't we just start over?" I offered. "Let me ask you a different question: Would you say that dying has been a relief for you, overall? Or, more generally: Is death a reprieve from the pain and suffering of being alive?"

The rumors claimed that the Summer Ghost was the spirit of a girl who committed suicide, after all—so assuming that was true, she must have done it for a reason. And what I wanted to know more than anything was...whatever those pains and anxieties she had might have been, was she released from them in death? Or would they gnaw away at her brain for all eternity? Aoi and Ryo seemed very interested to hear the answer to this as well, and we all waited on tenterhooks for her reply.

"I mean, I can't speak for *everyone*," Ayane started at last. "I'm sure it varies from person to person. But just speaking for myself, well..."

She trailed off for a moment, narrowing her eyes ever so slightly. I could only assume she was thinking back on her time amongst the living.

"No, let's not talk about me," she finally declared. "Who cares, honestly."

Just then, a soft orange glow crept up in the corner of my peripheral vision. The sparklers, still suspended in midair, began to shed sparks again—they traced trails of light that then burst and branched out into those telltale pine-needle patterns. Though slow at first, the sparkling was growing faster and more erratic by the second. The flow of time was rapidly returning to normal.

"The worlds of the living and the dead are trying to pull apart from each other once more," Ayane explained. "They can't overlap like this for long. It's time for us to go our separate ways."

"Wait, you're leaving us already?" asked Aoi. She clearly wasn't ready to call it a night just yet, but the Summer Ghost simply smiled softly and waved the three of us goodbye.

"It was nice talking to you all," Ayane said. "Bye now. Haunt you later."

Her peculiar farewell caught me a little off guard, but Aoi didn't miss a beat.

"Bye, Ayane-san!" she called out, waving back. "Haunt you later!"

The wind picked up, and the grass began to sway once more. As the buzzing insects resumed their flights, our sparklers fell to the asphalt and extinguished. I watched with my own two eyes as the ghost of Sato Ayane slipped away soundlessly into thin air—leaving the three of us stranded on the runway, too stunned to say a word.

Three

Summer Ghost

ALTHOUGH IT WAS summer vacation, there was still one day over the break when all students were required to come to school. It was our first time back on campus in weeks, and my classmates had been pretty rowdy over the course of the day—but now that they'd all gone home, the summer silence settled over the classroom once more.

"You still haven't made up your mind, then?" asked my homeroom teacher. He was seated across from me at the next desk over. He'd asked me to stay after class so we could talk about my higher education plans.

"No, sir," I said.

"Well, don't wait too long. With your academic prowess, I'm sure you could get in just about anywhere you applied."

In his hands, he held a results sheet for a mock entrance exam with my name on it. There were grades for each of the five tested subjects on a scale from A to E, and I had gotten all As. We had a one-on-one meeting about this before, back during the spring semester. As my guidance counselor, it was his job to help me figure out what path I'd be taking after graduation, what university I wanted to go to, and so forth. I didn't have any good answers for him then, and I still didn't have any answers for him now.

"I'm planning to talk it over with my mother and decide from there."

"Good. Try to come up with a shortlist of ideas before break's over, at least."

This entire conversation, of course, was premised on the assumption that I *would* be going to college after high school. And I could tell from his tone that he wanted me to apply for the most elite schools I could possibly be accepted to. After all, the more students he sent off to prestigious universities, the better it would reflect on him during his next performance review. Or at least I assumed that was his incentive.

"God, I wish they could all be as bright as you," he said with a sigh. "It'd make things *so* much easier for me."

After making my way away from campus, I hopped on the train and headed for home. Under the harsh August sun, the walk from the station to my apartment building would have been pretty brutal, were it not for the shelter provided by the row of big, shady trees that lined the sidewalk.

THREE

I strode past a roadside bench where a mother and father were sitting with their newborn baby. The family seemed very content. I wondered if there'd ever been a time when I was an infant that my family had been as happy as that. As far back as I could remember, my mother and father always fought. Then, when I was in late elementary school, they finally bit the bullet and got a divorce, and I had lived with only my mother ever since.

I took the elevator up to our floor and let myself into the apartment. My mother had to work late tonight, so I'd have the place to myself for several hours. After turning on the air conditioning in my bedroom, I changed out of my sweat-soaked uniform and into a fresh set of loungewear. Then, I opened up my closet and pulled out the sketchbook that I'd buried deep beneath my winter clothes. The most recent drawing inside was still the rough sketch I did of the Summer Ghost the other day, back at the café where I met up with Ryo and Aoi. It still amazed me how close the resemblance was to the real thing, despite me having drawn it before we even met Ayane.

Like a repressed Catholic hiding his rosary beneath the floorboards in the Tokugawa period of Japan, I hid my sketchbook deep in my closet to keep it safe from my mother's prying eyes. I knew that if she ever were to find it, she'd almost certainly throw it in the trash, just like she tossed my wooden easel, canvases, paints, and paintbrushes before I started high school. She wouldn't even let me keep the few award certificates I'd won. My mother claimed my art was only going to get in the way of my studies. She had no idea I was still drawing to this day behind her back—and if she found out, there'd be hell to pay.

I decided I would put on some music and do a few sketches to pass the time until my mother got home. I tried to make a habit of drawing as regularly as I could so as not to lose my touch and let my technical skills atrophy. I grabbed a soft-lead pencil and got to work, drawing lines across the page. First I sketched the three of us, making the trek over to the abandoned airfield. Then, I drew the runway as seen through a rusty chain-link fence, stretching off into the horizon. And finally, I drew Ayane, as best I could remember her.

It was only in retrospect that it finally sank in just how surreal that whole experience was—to the point that I almost wondered if it had merely been a particularly lucid dream. One that the three of us had somehow all experienced together. But no, the Summer Ghost really *did* exist, and we'd all had the chance to converse with her. I had proof to show for it too. Specifically, her name: Sato Ayane.

I looked her up online shortly after I made it home that night, thinking perhaps I might find some information as to who she really was, and sure enough, I quickly found mentions of a Sato Ayane that perfectly fit the bill. A twenty-year-old woman who went missing three years ago under mysterious circumstances—just weeks before the first reported sighting of the Summer Ghost. Assuming her disappearance was directly related to her death, the dates lined up almost perfectly. The apparition we met was no dream or hallucination, but an actual human being who lived and died right here in our neck of the woods.

It was already dark outside by the time I heard my mother walk in the front door. I snapped my sketchbook closed to stow it away, swept my loose pencils into a drawer, and joined her for dinner out at the dining room table. Our main dish for tonight was a smorgasbord of small, pre-prepared side dishes she picked up from the store on her way home. The only nights she actually cooked a full meal were ones when she got off work early, though I also made dinner for us from time to time.

"You had school today, didn't you?" she asked. "How'd that go?"

"Fine," I said. "Just normal."

"Normal meaning what? Elaborate."

My mother was a STEM major who'd been hired by one of the world's leading conglomerates after graduating college. She did not tolerate wishy-washy answers.

"Meaning that nothing interesting or out of the ordinary happened that would warrant additional discussion," I said.

As I watched my mother slowly nibble away at her food, I tried to imagine what her reaction would be upon learning I was dead. Would she even cry? Probably, I guessed. She'd think back on the good times, like when I was still in diapers, or maybe when I was in preschool or what have you and be overcome by a profound sense of loss. For all of the things I held against her, I did still harbor some amount of love for her as the woman who'd raised and nurtured me. And part of me did feel terrible for wanting to take the life she'd given me and leave her here without any family whatsoever.

After we finished eating, we discussed my higher education plan. She brought out her work laptop and pulled up a spreadsheet with all of my grades and test scores.

"You made a careless mistake on a single math problem that prevented you from getting a perfect score," she said. "That's unacceptable. Do better."

We went down the list, and she grilled me for the umpteenth time on each and every tiny mistake I made that could appear on my record. My mother never praised me, not even when I got all As. She considered that a form of coddling—and that if she told me I was performing well, I'd let it go to my head and get careless thereafter. All I could do was continue to play my role as her good little honor student, doing as best I could. Not to please her, but rather to ensure I never upset her. It hadn't always been this way, though. Back when I was in elementary school, I used to stand up for myself quite a bit more often.

However, every time I fought back, she'd respond in the same exact way. "I'm only telling this for your own good," she'd say. "I'm thinking about *your* future here. Because I want *you* to be happy."

Those were some of the only times she ever let glimpses of motherly concern peek through from beneath her clad iron veneer, and that alone was enough to make me feel bad for trying to stand up for myself. In the end, I'd always give in and do as she said due to some vague feeling of indebtedness or obligation as her son.

"I've picked out a few colleges that seem viable given your academics," she went on. "I've also got brochures for each of them, which you can look through later."

My mother had already sent away for various documentation from all of the potential colleges she selected, which were stacked in a big pile on the table. I might even have been glad to have her do so much of the work in planning out my future and choosing a college for me...were I a mindless puppet with no will of my own.

"Okay. I'll take a look and try to settle on a few," I said, picking up the pile of brochures. This response seemed to satisfy my mother, thankfully, and I let out an internal sigh of relief. Living with her was like something of a mental game that always kept me on my toes—but so long as I never picked the incorrect dialogue options during these interactions, I'd be able to go to sleep that night without drawing her ire or having to sit through another lecture.

I didn't loathe my mother, not by any means. I knew just how hard she worked, often late into the night at this very table, just to support our family and make ends meet. Sometimes, I'd even find her passed out asleep on the table with her laptop still open, and I'd go grab a cardigan to drape over her shoulders so she wouldn't catch a cold. I knew that her hypercritical nature when it came to me was just her own (admittedly backward) way of showing her love for me, and I did genuinely appreciate her concern. But a lot of the time, it was far more suffocating than it was helpful.

In her mind, she probably felt she was doing me a kindness by throwing away all of my beloved art supplies from junior high, thinking that if I kept pouring so much time into my hobbies, I'd be wasting valuable studying time and thus sabotaging my own future. My mother genuinely believed that if I failed my entrance exams, I'd be resigned to being a societal outcast for the rest of my life, only able to eke out a meager existence with low-paying grunt work. By her logic, there was simply no other option than to get rid of these distractions, once and for all.

My mother and I traded off after-dinner cleanup duties every other day. It was her turn to wash dishes today, so I went and took the first bath. The two of us generally spent the last hours of the night before bed doing our own separate things—only on very rare occasions did we sit on the couch and watch TV together.

When it came time to retire for the evening and I lay in bed waiting for sleep to take hold, my thoughts wandered back to my father once again. He was a very tall man—a gentle giant, as it were—whom I never saw lose his temper, not even once. Granted, it was entirely possible this impression of him had been colored, to a large degree, by just how ruthless my mother was in comparison during their many disagreements. He had a very good grasp of English and worked as a translator for a living. He apparently spent several years in America during his childhood, which I assumed had a lot to do with his high level of fluency. His parents had also had him baptized during this period of his life, and he had been a practicing Catholic ever since.

Not to imply that he was a particularly devout believer—I never even saw him say grace before a meal. He would go to mass on Sundays and make the occasional small offering to his church, but that was about it. I had no idea how important his faith was to him in reality, but I did assume that it came in handy (at least indirectly) for his translation work. Since nearly 75 percent of U.S. citizens identified as Christians, having a deep understanding of the Christian mindset and their beliefs no doubt gave him better insight into aspects of American culture that would otherwise seem quite inscrutable to an outside observer.

Given that my mother had always been a staunch atheist, I found it rather shocking in retrospect that she ever entertained the idea of being joined in holy matrimony with him, even if it had ultimately been short-lived. But even so, there was a time when the two of them were deeply in love, which I assumed made the prospect of marriage seem rather enticing despite their wildly different beliefs. Not to imply that my mother ever openly criticized him for his faith, to my knowledge—obviously, she knew better than to do that in a country that guaranteed religious freedom to all. The only thing she *did* do, as far as I could recall, was forbid him from taking me along to church on Sundays. She apparently felt quite strongly that it was not his right to indoctrinate me into Christianity, especially when I was far too young to make that decision for myself.

And so my father lived his life guided by God, and my mother lived hers guided by science—and for the initial honeymoon period of their marriage, they apparently *did* make a concerted effort to accept each other's beliefs. But it didn't last for long.

I distinctly remembered one instance toward the end of their marriage when my father wasn't around, and my mother let her true feelings show.

"Surely, he can't actually *believe* in any of that nonsense..." she had sneered. "Some divine, benevolent deity, just floating up there in the sky? Ridiculous..."

After the divorce papers were signed and it was decided that my father would have to move out, my mother wasted no time at all in disposing of his remaining effects, including the various religious ornaments he'd left sitting around the apartment. There was a small statue of the Virgin Mary he received from a member of his congregation, a decorative angel he brought back as a souvenir from one of his trips abroad... There had been so many colors, so many *things* in this apartment back when my father still lived here—and she got rid of every single one. Now this place was little more than a sterile, lifeless cage for the two of us to exist in together—a space for eating, sleeping, and nothing more.

Like my mother, I was also nonreligious. I never once entertained the notion of there being an almighty being. And even if I *had* been a believer at one point, the fact that I was now contemplating suicide should be proof enough that I wasn't anymore. Taking one's own life was considered a major taboo, not just in Christianity, but in all the world's major religions. To my knowledge, the act was generally considered to put an irremovable taint on one's soul in the next life. One of the fundamental tenets of Christianity, for example, was that life was a divine gift bestowed upon us by God, and to take one's own was to willfully squander that gift, thereby spitting in the face of God. The relatively high proportion of nonreligious people amongst the Japanese population was often cited as a major contributor to Japan's high suicide rate compared to the rest of the world.

Surely, if I held even the slightest hint of faith in my heart, then the mere thought of suicide would send shivers of fear and shame down my spine. If I believed that I owed my life to my creator like my father did, then I wouldn't even be considering this.

Owing my life to my creator... Gee, where have I heard that one before?

Indeed, that train of thought was almost eerily reminiscent of one of my mother's favorite stock comebacks, which she loved to whip out anytime she felt I was being too obstinate, or ungrateful, or combative.

"If I hadn't brought you into this world, you wouldn't even be here right now. Show a little gratitude, why don't you?"

That line of logic always struck me as a bit funny, because while I admittedly had no recollection of being born, I was fairly certain I had little say in the matter. But if I had my way, I'd at least make sure that when I died, it would be on my own terms. Not anyone else's.

During one of my break periods at cram school, I pulled out my smartphone and started a new group DM with Aoi and Ryo. We talked for a while about the surreal experience we all shared the other day.

"Guess ghosts really are *real, huh,"* wrote Aoi. *"Kinda spooky to think about it now that I had time to dwell on it."*

Apparently, her fear of the supernatural had only gotten worse—which seemed odd to me initially, given how well she and Ayane had hit it off. However, it seemed to be more the thought of less-friendly ghosts that could hypothetically be lurking in any random dark corridor that was giving her anxiety as of late.

Ryo, on the other hand, seemed to have achieved a whole new level of inner peace. *"Me? I couldn't be less afraid after meeting her. Hell, I'm grateful. Now I'm not so afraid of dying anymore,"* he wrote. *"What's your take on it, Tomoya?"*

"Don't really have one, honestly," I replied. *"If anything, I just wish we could've had more time to talk with her. Wanted to know more about what comes after death—though I guess she did say she doesn't know a whole lot about it herself."*

She led us to believe that she'd been in a sort of purgatory state, wandering aimlessly around this general area as a ghost ever since she died. She also claimed that she had yet to encounter even a single other dead person, and that she figured they'd all been sent on to the next life without her. If we assumed that this world and the next one really did exist on two totally separate "layers" of existence, then it stood to reason that perhaps she had been left behind somewhere in between—which would explain why she only became visible to us while the two layers briefly overlapped each other, thereby bridging it.

After talking about the Summer Ghost for a while, the three of us switched over to more mundane conversation topics. Aoi had apparently been spending her summer break cooped up in her bedroom doing nothing but playing video games all day. Ryo had been going back and forth from the hospital pretty much nonstop. He had a whole cocktail of drugs he needed to take each day. It sounded really rough.

"What about you, Tomoya-kun? What have you been up to lately?" asked Aoi.

"Cram school," I replied. *"All day, every day. Those entrance exams aren't gonna study for themselves."*

During this time of year, when most college hopefuls were on summer vacation, most cram schools ran special, extra-hardcore short courses for people like me. They ran from morning to night, and you studied until your eyes started to bleed from staring at workbook problems all day.

"What's even the point, dude?" Ryo asked bluntly. *"I mean, you're just gonna off yourself anyway, right? Why go through the stress of studying for exams?"*

"For real!" Aoi agreed. *"If I were you, I'd totally ditch. I mean, who needs studying where we're going? Screw that noise!"*

They did have a point. If I really *was* going to kill myself, then there was certainly no point in studying for entrance exams I'd never take.

"Don't waste what little time you have left doing mindless bookwork, my dude," wrote Ryo. *"Spend it doing stuff you actually* like *to do."*

"Hard to argue with that coming from a guy in your position," I admitted.

Still, part of me felt it best to continue living my life like normal up until the very day I chose to end it all. If I started slacking off and enjoying myself now, my mother was sure to notice, and that would only make things harder in the long run. As such, my current plan was to continue playing the role of the dutiful honor student for her until I had everything I needed to commit suicide all planned out and ready to go.

On the private message boards where the three of us first met, you'd occasionally see recruitment threads pop up in which people attempted to arrange mass suicides with anyone and everyone that was interested. But the three of us hadn't even discussed that as an option. As of right now, we were all planning to do the deed separately—on our own time and in our own respective ways.

"So, when are you two planning on dying?" I asked the room. *"I figure I'll probably do it sometime around the end of the year. Wouldn't want to overlap too closely with you guys."*

"Wait, why can't we all just do it on the same day?" asked Ryo.

"Well, if we spread it out, then those of us who are left can at least go to the others' funerals. Thought that might be kinda nice," I answered.

"Wait, don't tell me... Are you the obsessive, gotta-have-everything-planned-out-months-in-advance, right-down-to-the-minute type, Tomoya-kun?" asked Aoi.

"I take it you're not?"

"I kinda wanna wait and see what the weather's like the morning of, before I decide for sure. I mean, you only die once, right? Might as well pick a nice day to do it, then, if I've got the choice. Feel like I could rest nice and easy beneath a big blue sky."

Just then, my cram school instructor walked back into the classroom, and all of the other students who were hanging around talking to one another quieted and returned to their seats. I slid my smartphone back into my backpack. After the instructor handed out the next worksheet, the only sound to be heard in the classroom for the next hour was the frantic scribbling of pencils.

Being the middle of summer, it was still relatively light outside after cram school let out. I'd gotten a text from my mother letting me know that she expected to be home very late tonight. I waffled back and forth for a few moments as to whether I should just head straight home and make the most of my alone time or not—but in the end, I settled on making a second trip out to the abandoned airfield. I stopped by the hardware store to buy a small set of fireworks, hopped on the bus, and watched out the window as it carried me away from the city into remnants of suburban sprawl that became more and more bleak.

I wanted to speak with the Summer Ghost again. It was a spur-of-the-moment impulse based on my mother's text, so I didn't bother asking Aoi and Ryo if either of them wanted to come. We didn't even know if it was *possible* for the same person to encounter her more than once yet, after all. For all we knew, her appearing to us the other day could have been a one-time, freak occurrence. This was another reason I felt compelled to go back—pure curiosity as to how the phenomenon worked.

I hopped off the bus at the edge of the prefecture and got to walking. It was still pretty hot out as I trudged my way up the unpaved road, but I soon found myself at the top of the hill, staring down at the giant airfield surrounded by a rusty old chain-link fence. Just like last time, I slipped into the lot via the break in the fence and made my way through the tall grass to the crack-ridden pavement of the runway. I put down my backpack and got straight to work unwrapping the set of fireworks I bought on the way.

Last time, she only appeared after we'd gone through all of our other fireworks and were down to only a single pack of Japanese-style sparklers. This led me to wonder if perhaps these were the only fireworks that could summon her, so I tried using a more universal torch-style sparkler first to test this theory. It was a morning glory, a type that shot forth a powerful spray of multicolored sparks—pink, green, and blue—from the end of a stick for about thirty seconds or so before fizzling out. As the half-light faded and dusk began to fall, its dazzling array of colors almost seemed to pierce straight through the descending veil of night.

But the Summer Ghost did not appear.

Next, I pulled out one of the Japanese-style sparklers and held my lighter up to the bottom tip to set it aglow. In seconds, the gunpowder combusted, and the chemical reaction of potassium sulfate, potassium carbonate, and sulfuric acid created a viscous blob that soon swelled up into a molten, spherical slag. And it was within this glowing red orb, which almost seemed to radiate with the fragile flicker of life itself, that tiny pockets of unstable gas began to build up in the form of countless bubbles. When these finally burst, they sent tiny droplets of white-hot mist spraying out from it—and it was these microscopic beads of molten matter that we called sparks.

These pinpricks of light left trails in the air as they flew out in their initial arcs, then burst due to even further chemical reactions within the droplet into even tinier sparks, which then fired off in all directions to form those branching, pine-needle patterns we knew so well. It was a softer, warmer sort of sparkle than you could get from any other type of handheld firework.

If you were to stop time and examine any individual instant of this dazzling phenomenon from one millisecond to the next, you'd be looking at nothing more than a series of simple chemical reactions, all of which science could easily explain. And yet we humans had the uncanny ability to perceive within them a kind of beauty—an allegory for the fragile, fluctuating nature of our own lives that moved us deep down inside, often with a profound sense of melancholy toward the ephemeral. It was the sort of thing that, just by watching it, could stir up deep emotions from within our hearts. If you asked me, it was this very ability to appreciate these inexplicable, abstract forms of beauty that made us human—and this was a feeling I often tried to capture by depicting these same, seemingly mundane yet highly evocative things in my own artwork from time to time.

Before long, the sparks crackled and danced with even greater fervor.

Then, the singing of insects grew distant, and the wind blowing through the grass went still.

Out of the corner of my eye, I perceived a sudden contrast. A human form.

And there she stood—a pale specter, set against the dark.

I wondered why exactly, of all things, it was fireworks that caused the Summer Ghost to appear. I knew, of course, that in ancient times they were thought to have supernatural properties that could appease the dead. It was also said that the reason there were so many fireworks festivals held in the summer months was because they were a natural evolution of the okuribi ritual traditionally done as a part of Obon, the Japanese festival of the dead. This was a custom in which a large bonfire, or "guiding fire," was lit to help send the returning spirits of deceased ancestors safely back to the afterlife after having wandered out to visit their homelands once more. Supposedly, every fireworks festival in the country owed its origins to this ancient ritual of seeing off lost loved ones.

Perhaps the fireworks we lit here at the abandoned airfield had a similar but opposite effect for wandering souls like Ayane's—a light to guide her safely down to the earth, like runway beacons for airplanes in the night.

Ayane walked over and crouched down in front of me, gazing wistfully into the sparkler's light. "How pretty. You know, I always loved these things," she said.

Neither her footsteps nor the rustling of her clothes made a sound. She was right there before my very eyes, and yet it was like she wasn't there at all—her existence was so faint that she threatened to vanish like a wisp of smoke at any moment. After a few more beads of light dust burst forth from the droplet at the bottom of the sparkler, they froze in midair like tiny stars in orbit around a single, bright red sun.

"Tomoya-kun," she started, her face illuminated in the dark by the orange glow. As I watched it cast shadows across her face, I wondered if this interaction of light meant that she and I now inhabited the same space, subject to the same physical phenomena, or if it was simply a figment of my perception. "Why have you come back here?"

"I had some other questions I wanted to ask you," I answered, my voice cracking. I thought I came mentally prepared, but apparently I still wasn't level-headed enough to remain perfectly calm in the face of a ghostly presence.

Ayane ran her fingers through her bangs, pulling them back out of her face—offering a rare glimpse of her porcelain-pale neck in the process. "Hopefully nothing too esoteric this time," she said.

"Well, the thing is...I've been thinking about killing myself," I confessed. "As have the other two who were here with me the other day."

"Yeah, I kind of had a feeling."

"Oh... You did?" I asked.

"You all had that look about you—like you'd already resigned yourselves to dying. Even for all Aoi-chan's pep, she couldn't hide the darkness lurking deep within her eyes. Not from me, anyway. Also, it seems I don't appear as clearly to people who are in a sound and healthy state of mind. From what I can tell, they either see me as almost entirely translucent, or just a blurry, featureless mannequin. You kids are the first who've been able to see me crystal clear and have an actual, intelligible interaction with me. And I'm certain that's because you've all become captivated by death."

"Please, I want to know more about what death is like," I said. "Could you tell me a bit more about your personal experience? What did it feel like? Was it as bad as people say?"

"Oh, it was terrifying. Excruciating, even. So if you're asking my advice, then I really wouldn't recommend doing so voluntarily. There's no need to take matters into your own hands. Just live your life. Don't worry—it'll still come for you in the end. It always does."

"It's already excruciating enough just being alive," I remarked. "If it means ending the pain once and for all, then why not just bite the bullet and get it over with, I say."

"But *why* is your life so excruciating, Tomoya-kun?"

"I wish I could tell you. All I know is that I'm sick and tired of it all, and I really can't go on like this much longer."

Ayane let out a deep, exasperated sigh. "See, I blame our dysfunctional society for this," she said. "It's like a factory designed to churn out good little worker bees, but all it does is make apathetic robots out of bright young kids like you."

"Are we really extrapolating my own personal suffering into a more generalized rant on modern society right now?"

"Well, what other explanation is there? When you can't pinpoint the source of a problem, you just blame it on society as a whole. Everyone knows that."

"That's a pretty transparent cop-out," I said.

"I mean, I'm a ghost. What did you expect?"

I had to admit, it was a solid retort—even if it did nothing to support her argument. Really, I just admired the sheer flippancy of it.

"So what's next for you, Ayane-san?" I asked. "You gonna try to reach nirvana one of these days, or just stay in limbo?"

"Reach nirvana...?" she asked. "I don't know what that means."

"Oh, sorry. It's a Buddhist term, originally—for achieving enlightenment, or a state of 'Buddhahood'—that is, true inner peace. But nowadays it's used more colloquially as a synonym for making it to heaven, or paradise, or whatever you might call the next life. The main reason I used it was because I figured maybe your soul's not at peace yet and that's why you're stuck wandering around here as a lonely ghost."

"I see. You know, for a high school kid, you sure do know an awful lot of random trivia, Tomoya-kun. I don't think most kids your age are that familiar with Buddhism," Ayane said. "Hey, so tell me, do you think there really *is* a heaven out there? 'Cause I sure don't. Me, I think we just die and disappear and that's it."

"That's quite the take, coming from someone in your predicament," I said, not entirely sure if she was being serious or not. But assuming she truly believed that, then what exactly did she even think she *was* right now? "Ayane-san, please stop living in denial and accept the fact that you're a ghost already."

Her lips curled up into a playful little smirk. "You're so uptight, Tomoya-kun."

"I'm an honor student. Comes with the territory."

"You should try being a ghost for a while. Maybe that'd help loosen you up."

Ayane had been crouched down this entire time to get a closer view of the sparkler, but now she shot back up to her feet. She clapped me gently on the shoulders. I assumed that since she was a ghost, her hands would just go straight through me—but they didn't. There wasn't much force at all, but I could clearly feel myself being pushed slightly off balance.

Try being a ghost? Loosen me up?

As my mind reeled in confusion, my vision blurred. There was an odd, momentary floating sensation, and I felt a sinking in my stomach—like when you lose your footing on a slippery floor or misjudge the number of remaining steps on a staircase. As soon as I realized I was falling backward, I scrambled to regain my balance—but as soon as I did, I found myself staring at the back of someone's head from mere inches away.

And it wasn't Ayane's head—it was my own. Somehow, I was now watching myself—Sugisaki Tomoya, sparkler still in hand—from a third-person view.

It was an *extremely* unsettling feeling, and I immediately felt nauseous.

"Wh-what in the hell did you just do?!" I demanded.

"Relax," said Ayane. "I just plucked your soul from its vessel, that's all."

"...Well, can you put it back? Please?"

"I will. Later."

She grabbed me by the hand with frigid but soft fingers. This one touch alone was enough to make her once-illusory presence feel that much more tangible in my head. Now that my soul had been divorced from my body, she and I were no different from one another. And in this new form, I felt light as air—released from the bonds of gravity.

"Come on," she said. "Let's go."

Ayane took off running, dragging me along by the hand. I was still quite a bit flustered, but all I could do was find my footing and follow suit. We raced down the runway and eventually, our feet left the ground. Before I could even register what was happening, we were floating in midair, sprinting up into the night sky. I took one last look back at my body where we'd left it on the runway as we kissed the earth goodbye.

And then that was that—we were officially in flight.

We floated higher and higher into the sky—so effortlessly that it almost felt like we were being sucked into the stratosphere. I couldn't even feel the wind pressure around me.

"Take a look," said Ayane, still holding me firmly by the hand.

I looked down and watched as the abandoned airfield fell further and further away from us. I could see suburban neighborhoods, river floodplains, and city lights across the distant horizon. We couldn't have been more than a hundred meters above the ground, but it was still high enough to make my entire body shiver with fright.

"H-how are we even floating like this?" I asked. "Is there some sort of trick to it?"

"I just imagined us flying and my mind did the rest," she told me. "We can go in any direction we want just by picturing it in our heads."

Ayane led me by the hand as we glided through the sky beneath the pale moonlight. We could go as fast or as slow as we wanted—not even inertia had any hold over us. No matter how fast or how wildly we flew, we never had to stop to catch our breath, nor did we have to close our eyes to shield them from the wind. Before long, we had flown far enough away from the airfield that we were soaring above the station, way back in the commercial district.

Is this really happening right now?

"Hold tight. We're going in," she said.

I looked up and saw that we were barreling straight toward a large office building. Thinking we were about to crash, I braced myself for impact—but then we passed straight through its outer walls, then through corridors and offices where so many businesspeople were still hard at work, and then right out the other side of the building. Apparently, while we were in ghost form, not even physical barriers posed an obstacle to us.

"How 'bout *that*, Tomoya-kun?" Ayane said, wearing the smuggest of grins.

"You could do some serious corporate espionage like this," I mused.

"Heck, you can even peek inside bank vaults if you want to—not that you can really do anything with what's inside. It's hard to pull off a heist when you can't touch anything."

It seemed like there was little she could do to interfere with the world of the living.

"Pretty much the only things I *can* touch are souls like yours, which are more or less halfway dead already," she explained. "It's only because your mind's become so captivated by death that I was able to whisk you away like this."

Up there in the ether above our city, Ayane slowed to a stop. Together, we gazed down at the crowds of people frozen down on the streets below—the bustling pedestrians crossing the street to wherever it was they needed to go were now trapped in stasis.

"Now you try," she said. "See if you can fly on your own."

"Huh?"

As Ayane relinquished her grip on my hand and floated a short distance away, my stomach dropped—and, having nothing to hold on to, I immediately went into freefall. My vision started spinning and I could see the ground beneath me growing rapidly closer by the second. All I could do was cry out in terror as I tumbled along the side of a tall building toward the asphalt. I braced myself for impact, and the moment I hit the pavement, my vision went dark—like someone had pulled the plug. It was more or less how I always envisioned it looking whenever I fantasized about jumping from a tall rooftop, only now I was actually experiencing it for myself.

And yet to my surprise, the asphalt did not stop me. My soul kept going—entering the street and tumbling underground. I panicked—it felt a bit like I just did a cannonball into a deep pool. I thrashed my limbs about, struggling to find my way back to the surface. It wasn't like I was drowning or suffocating, per se (there was no need to breathe in this state to begin with)—it was more that I simply no longer knew which way was up and was desperate to regain my bearings.

It really did look and feel as though I fell into a deep pool of murky water—and although the concrete and mud I was passing through beneath the ground were obscuring my vision, it seemed as though I could perceive my surroundings through some other sense. I could tell, more or less, where I was underground in relation to all of the manmade structures that were also down on this level, like building foundations, underground shopping malls, and whatnot. However, my range of perception in that regard didn't reach very far.

"You're okay, Tomoya-kun. Don't panic," said Ayane. She grabbed me by the arm as I wriggled and squirmed like a blind worm in the dirt. Apparently she'd followed me down into the earth. With her now pulling me up, I was able to stabilize my posture. After giving me a chance to regain my bearings, she dragged me back up to the surface.

"What in the hell was *that* for?!" I shouted.

"I just wanted to see you freak out a little bit, that's all," she said. "I mean, who doesn't relish the chance to see a usually-calm-and-collected type lose their cool for once? It's almost titillating in a way, y'know what I mean? ...Well, I guess maybe a guy like you wouldn't understand."

"You're correct. I do *not* understand, nor do I have any desire to."

"Look, I'm sorry, okay? Here, I'll teach you how to actually fly now, so cheer up."

We soared up into the skies over the city once more. She gave me a moment to calm down before grabbing both my hands so that we were floating facing each other.

"Remember, gravity has no effect on you as a ghost," she said. "You're free to go and fly off in whatever direction you want to. All you have to do is picture it clearly in your mind's eyes, and I promise you won't fall."

This time, she let go of my hands much more slowly—and while I still did panic and lose a bit of altitude at first, once I took Ayane's advice and scrambled to imagine myself floating alongside her, I managed to catch my own fall and float back up to her level.

"Whoa, hey!" I shouted. "I'm actually doing it!"

"See, there you go," said Ayane.

After another few minutes' practice, I was propelling my soul here and there across the skyline like it was no trouble at all. Ayane really wasn't kidding: all you had to do was picture a direction in your head, and off you went.

"Now then," said Ayane, calling out to me from beneath the moonlight. "Where would you like to go next? Just pick a destination and make a wish."

On the outskirts of town was a vast nature park that also housed an art museum on its grounds. It was already well past closing time, so the doors were locked—but that hardly made a difference for me and Ayane. We slipped through its outer walls, right past the night security guard stationed outside the building, and snuck our way into the museum. With no visitors inside, the lights in each of the museum's wings had been turned off for the night. The only illumination remaining was the green glow of the emergency exit signs and an occasional bright red dot here and there where the fire alarms were located. We could have easily flown down the halls, but for whatever reason, we opted to walk slowly and respectfully like proper museum guests.

"Over here," I said to Ayane. "This is the intended route."

"You come here pretty often?" she asked.

"Used to. My dad took me here a lot when I was a kid."

One of the museum staff members was of the same faith as my father, so we were treated like family any time we came here. There were several pieces of Christian art on display here, including an old Russian icon of Jesus Christ and an original oil painting depicting the Annunciation from somewhere in Europe. My father would sometimes stop in front of these art pieces and relate some anecdotes from the Bible to me.

"I've definitely never been here after closing time, though," I added. "It's kind of surreal. I used to dream about getting to stay here after hours and look at all the artwork as long as I liked with no other museum visitors to disturb me."

"You're a pretty big art buff, aren't you, Tomoya-kun?" she asked while standing beside the statue of a woman on display at the center of the gallery and attempting to strike the same pose.

"Not sure I'd go quite that far, but I *was* in the art club back in junior high. My fellow clubmates and I used to come here pretty often too."

Though all of the lights in the building were off, if I really strained my eyes, I could still make out even the smaller details of the paintings on display. I perceived them through some alternate form of vision I had right now that wasn't dependent on light whatsoever. I examined each painting from point-blank range—close enough that I'd be issued a warning from one of the security guards under normal circumstances. I could even dip my face into the painting itself if I wanted to and examine the microscopic contours of each and every brush stroke along the canvas.

"Look, Tomoya-kun. I'm royalty now."

Ayane had seen fit to float up into the massive oil portrait of some aristocratic woman and poke her head out from behind the canvas, superimposing her own face right over where the subject's would otherwise be—almost like one of those photo op boards with the faces cut out that you could find at any tourist trap. I was genuinely impressed by her ingenuity; not everyone would be able to come up with such a dumb way to take advantage of their incorporeality.

As we talked while we walked through the dusky corridors, we eventually came to the aforementioned oil painting my father loved so much. It depicted the Annunciation—a moment from the New Testament in which an angel visits the Virgin Mary and informs her of her destiny to give birth to the savior of mankind through the miracle of Immaculate Conception.

"I have to say, I'm a little surprised to hear you were in art club," said Ayane. "You don't really strike me as the artsy type, Tomoya-kun."

"Why's that?" I asked.

"Well, I mean, art's all about feeling and intuition, right? Expressing yourself through emotion above all else. You seem more like someone who thinks much more critically and values hard facts and logic over your own feelings. I know this is only the second time we've talked, but just based on my first impressions, you give off *serious* STEM major vibes. Like, I could see you meticulously sketching out blueprints all night, but painting portraits? Not so much."

"You actually need a pretty logical mindset to be a good artist, I'd say."

"Is that right?" she asked.

"Yeah, and not just in drawing or painting. The same goes for sculpting and music too, I'm pretty sure. It might all seem like pure emotion and artistic talent at first blush, but if you actually take a closer look, you'd find that there's a surprising amount of science behind your favorite art."

"Can you give me an example?"

"Well, let's say you're trying to choose what colors of paint to use in a painting," I began. "Just in terms of the bare basics, there's all sorts of color-related theories and diagrams that you can map out to figure out what shades will look best with one another, or make the best contrast, which you can triangulate via color triad, and so on... Stuff like that."

"Wow," she said. "That all sounds *really* boring."

"Well, there's more to it than that, of course. Say you were going to paint a sunflower, for instance. What color would you want to use for the background?"

"Something that would make the yellow stand out, I guess? Like blue or green?"

"You'd think so, right? But one of Vincent van Gogh's *Sunflowers* pieces sold at auction to a Japanese insurance magnate to the tune of 5.8 billion yen, and that one used *yellow* for its background."

"Wait, so it was yellow on yellow?"

"Yep. And we all agree *that's* great art, so there must be something to it, right?"

The oil painting of the Annunciation in front of us used a mixture of bright blues and reds for the Virgin Mary's garb—she wore red clothes with a blue hooded cape. This was a fairly common representation of the Virgin Mary, but it was also a color scheme you saw very frequently in American comics, for instance. Some might argue that it was due in part to those being patriotic colors used in the American flag, but it could also very well be that there was something inherently "transcendent" about that particular color combination.

"There was a friend of mine in that art club who was *extremely* talented but didn't care one bit about artistic theory and whatnot," I added. "They just believed in the images they envisioned in their head as though they were absolute—sacred, almost—and painted them through that faith in their vision alone."

"And I take it you were the exact opposite type?" asked Ayane.

"Well, I guess I just didn't have their level of confidence. I'd spend forever studying composition and trying to map out my paintings all proportionally in accordance with time-honored techniques. Like, whenever I drew a human subject, I'd pull out a ruler and make sure that the sum of the lengths of their arms and shoulders was equal to their height."

"What's the point of that?"

"Well, because if you measure a real human, with their arms outstretched from fingertip to fingertip, you'll find that the length is almost exactly as wide as that person is tall," I explained, stretching my own arms wide out to indicate. "It's called your 'wingspan,' basically. If you've ever seen Leonardo da Vinci's *Vitruvian Man*, that's a pretty good illustration of this concept."

"And you're *always* thinking about stuff like this when you draw?" she asked. "Are you trying to make paintings or anatomy diagrams here?"

"It's just a little trick you can use to give your artwork better and more realistic proportions. That's all."

"So what was it that got you into painting in the first place?"

"I like to cite this one time back in elementary school. My mother and father both heaped loads of praise on me for a particular painting I'd done. That almost *never* happened, so it kind of stuck with me, I guess."

We entered paintings we did in class into a big art competition for our age group, and mine just so happened to win an award. That made both of my parents very, very happy. They were so proud of my achievement that they didn't even argue with one another a single time that day, and for once, I got to experience the illusion of living in a happy family. It meant a lot to me at the time, and in retrospect, was probably why I kept on painting—an attempt to gain their continued approval.

Ayane and I spent a good while wandering around the museum and appreciating each exhibit in the dark before finally heading back outside. Upon exiting the building, I half-expected to be hit by a crisp, cool breeze, or perhaps the strong scent of evergreens—but no such luck. Being a ghost was a bland, flavorless form of existence.

We rose up into the night sky once more with the moon still hanging brightly over us. We passed by a few pigeons, frozen in flight, as we made our way up to a steel radio tower standing in the middle of the forest, and then perched ourselves up on one of its upper beams, sitting side by side. This was merely an illusion, of course, because if we let gravity do its work, our legs would pass right through the steel. But since we imagined ourselves sitting on it, our weightless bodies were fixed in place.

Ayane gazed off into the distance, where the nightscape of our familiar city dotted the horizon with a thousand tiny pinpricks of light. "Pretty, isn't it?" she said. "Like you took a sky full of stars and anchored each one down to the earth."

"There's probably even more of them than our eyes can see right now, just considering how time has slowed to a stop," I pointed out. "LEDs and fluorescent lights, for example, only work by flickering rapidly on and off. A good portion of those must've been frozen in an unilluminated state."

"Why can't you just shut up and enjoy the beauty of it for what it is?"

I turned and looked over at her, glimpsing at her face from the side. Set against the full darkness of the night, her pale, lifeless skin stood out more prominently than ever.

Figuring this was probably the best opportunity I would get, I finally asked her a question that had been gnawing at my brain for days. The one thing I just couldn't reconcile.

"Why did you kill yourself, Ayane-san?"

She ran her fingers up through her hair, then back along her scalp. As her bangs fell back into place, she let out a sigh of resignation.

"I didn't kill myself," she said.

"So you're telling me that's the one thing the rumors got wrong, then? Even though they were right about everything else?" I asked.

"I don't know what to tell you. Maybe someone figured it would make the story more interesting, so they tacked on that little detail and everyone else ran with it."

"Wow. And here I convinced myself that we were kindred spirits. I looked up to you, even, as someone who actually managed to do the deed. I was going to ask your advice on preferred methods and everything."

"Yeah, sorry. Afraid I can't be of much help to you there," Ayane said.

"I guess I did find it a little strange though—with how you're still listed as a missing person on the National Police Agency website."

"Oh, yeah. Probably because they never found my body," she said nonchalantly—as though it were nothing. Like we were just making simple small talk. "I was murdered, basically."

Four

Summer Ghost

THE NEXT DAY, I made plans to meet up with Ryo and Aoi at a diner not far from the station. Luckily, they were both able to make it despite the short notice.

Aoi who showed up first. "Long time no see, Tomoya-kun," she said, walking over to the table.

"Hey," I said, lifting one hand to greet her. "Yeah, guess it's been a while... Doesn't *feel* all that long though, since we've been messaging back and forth every day."

"You don't have cram school today?"

"Figured I could afford to skip out for once," I replied.

Aoi ordered a fountain drink, and then went and got herself a melon soda. She took a few sips as we made idle chitchat until Ryo walked through the door. He quickly spotted our table, walked over, and took a seat next to Aoi. He immediately took off his hat and started fanning himself with it. The summer swelter was brutal today and you could practically feel each individual ray of sunlight piercing your skin.

Today, though, Ryo seemed awfully haggard and pale. I wondered to myself if his already poor bill of health made the heat that much more unbearable. I went over to the drink counter and poured an iced coffee for him.

"Sorry for calling you here on such short notice," I said. "Hope I didn't put you guys out too much."

"It's cool, dude," said Ryo. "Had to go to the hospital this morning anyway, so I was already out and about."

"Everything okay?" Aoi asked him.

"Honestly, I'm not doing super. Still just delaying the inevitable with meds, basically," he answered, then turned to face me. "Anyway, Tomoya—what'd you wanna talk about?"

"Well, there's something I think you guys deserve to know," I began. "Basically, I went back to the abandoned airfield last night, and..."

I told them all about my experience the previous evening—how I summoned the Summer Ghost once again using a sparkler, and how she divorced my soul from my body and took me on a flight through the night sky. I had to admit it all sounded rather fantastical, so I was a little worried they might think I hallucinated the whole thing.

Skepticism was painted all across Ryo's face. "You two went *flying* together? You're kidding me, right?"

"I believe it. I mean, if ghosts can fly, then it only makes sense that he could too, if she put him into soul form," said Aoi. She seemed somewhat enthralled by the idea. "Wow... Now I'm almost *excited* to die, ha ha. I better hurry up and kill myself, huh?"

"C'mon, dude. Don't say stuff like that," said Ryo, less than amused.

"Flying *was* pretty fun though, I gotta say. But that's not what I really called you guys here to talk about. You see, the thing is...Ayane-san can't give us any advice when it comes to killing ourselves. Because, apparently, she *didn't* commit suicide."

And so I proceeded to tell them what Ayane told me the night before—about her death and how it really happened.

Shortly after our conversation on the radio tower, Ayane told me there was somewhere else she wanted to take me. And so we zipped over residential streets like shooting stars, eventually soaring up the hill to a particularly wealthy neighborhood that looked down over the whole city. Toward the center of this well-to-do community was a lot upon which an old, Victorian-style manor stood—and it was there that we made our landing. Moths had gathered around the softly glowing porch lights, which were fashioned in the style of antique lanterns.

"What's this?" I asked.

"My old house," said Ayane. "Though now it's just my mom living here, all by herself. Come on in."

And with that, she passed right through the front door and vanished. I followed her inside shortly thereafter and found myself in a hushed foyer. I could almost smell the aging hardwood of the sturdy pillars and carved handrail snaking its way along the stairs.

Light leaked in through the opened door of what appeared to be the living room. I poked my head inside and saw an older woman reclining on the sofa reading a book of some sort. She had an air about her that reminded me a lot of Ayane—and the two looked quite similar in the face as well. I could only presume that this was her mother. She was wearing rather subdued attire dyed in muted tones.

"She's always reading at this hour," said Ayane. "Even back when I was still living here, this was how she preferred to spend her evenings."

Ayane loomed over her mother from behind the sofa—but the woman didn't notice either of our presences. She kept her eyes trained on whatever line of text she was currently reading. There was a large picture frame hung on the wall—a photo of a younger Ayane, back when she was still alive. Given that the police still officially had her listed as a missing person, there was a good chance this poor woman still believed her daughter might be out there somewhere, still alive.

Ayane reached out and laid her ghostly hand gently on top of her mother's. "She and I got into an argument that night, three years ago," she said. "It wasn't even worth getting upset about, looking back on it. We were just talking about what I was planning to do with myself after graduating from college. When the conversation took a turn that I didn't like, I just ran out of the house in a huff."

As she recounted this to me, she turned away from her mother and headed into the next room. I obediently followed suit.

"It was pretty stupid of me, honestly. I see that now in hindsight. But at the time, I guess I just let my emotions get the better of me, and I ran out into the wind and rain despite the fact that there was literally a typhoon coming in."

She ascended the staircase, going by a small window from which a few scant rays of moonlight came trickling in. I followed her down the second-floor hallway, past some impressionist paintings and a number of wooden doors. Eventually, she stopped in front of one of them and invited me to enter, so I did.

I could tell this had been Ayane's room—left untouched with all its furnishings and the bed still made for the past three years, presumably, aside from the thin white linens draped over some of the furnishings to prevent them from collecting dust.

Ayane seemed wistful as she looked around the room.

"I just kept on going, running right through the storm without so much as an umbrella," she continued. "Growing up, there was only ever one place I would go at times like that—the old neighborhood library. It was past closing time, but I figured that maybe I could at least take shelter from the rain beneath its eaves and wait out the storm. But just as I was crossing the street, I saw two blinding white lights come barreling toward me through the rain."

"Headlights, I'm guessing?"

"Yeah. Some car ran a red light probably, since I had the right of way. All I remember is the light getting brighter and brighter, and then all at once, a massive shock ran through my body...but I didn't die from the initial impact. I actually remember coming to, lying there on the asphalt—but everything was so hazy. I couldn't move my body, or even tell if I was in pain or not, really. Then, through my blurred vision, I saw the silhouette of a man step out from the driver's side door and start walking toward me where I lay..."

At this point in her explanation, Ayane walked over to her desk, crouched down, and crawled through the chair into the leg space beneath it. I couldn't imagine why, but she was now peeking out at me from underneath her desk, sitting with her legs hugged tight to her chest.

"When I next awoke, I found myself trapped in a tiny little space like this. It was probably a big suitcase, or at least that's my theory. Like one of those oversized ones designed for long vacations. I could tell from the composition and texture of the interior fabrics. It seemed like the driver curled me up into a ball and zipped me up inside—I couldn't move an inch."

"Jesus..." I muttered. "What kind of monster..."

"He probably mistook me for dead, I'm guessing. He thought he already killed me, so he threw me in his trunk and drove off to bury the evidence."

"Wait... He *buried* you?"

"Oh, yeah. That part was pretty terrifying. I could hear him piling the dirt on top of me and everything. I tried pounding on the lid of the suitcase and calling out for help, but it didn't do me any good. I was too weak to hit very hard, and could barely choke out anything more than a pathetic groan... Even so, I strained my ears and listened for any indication that he could hear me. All I could make out though was the sound of other cars passing by. I guess he must have buried me pretty close to the roadway or something. But anyway, yeah—it was just that and the sound of him shoveling dirt until eventually there wasn't enough oxygen left for me to breathe. At that point, my consciousness started to fade...

and that's the last thing I can remember. And then I was dead. Just like that."

Ayane rose to her feet once more, phasing right through the desk.

"The next thing I knew, I was drifting through the sky, looking down at the city below. To this day, my body still hasn't been found. I know that from watching my mom go about her days. She's still waiting for me to come home."

She cast her gaze down to the ground, her expression despondent. When I imagined how it must feel, as a mother, to hold out hope that your daughter was still alive for years when you knew the odds were greatly stacked against you, I couldn't help but empathize with her. A stabbing pang of sorrow shot through my chest.

"Do you know where you were buried?" I asked.

"I don't, unfortunately," replied Ayane. "I looked all over, but eventually gave up. It wasn't like finding my body would change anything, after all. Can't very well dig myself up or make a police report as a ghost, now, can I?"

She then slipped through the curtained window and back outside. I followed suit, and we now stood on the rooftop, with the starry night sky as our only backdrop.

"It's pretty depressing sometimes, though," she said. "I mean, I had so much left I wanted to do with my life...like go out and see the world, you know?"

"Isn't traveling one of the few things you still *can* do? Heck, you don't even have to pay for airfare anymore."

"Well, you've got me there," she said, narrowing her eyes in amusement—but the gesture belied the sorrow and resignation I could still sense deep within her. "Come on, Tomoya-kun. Let's get you back in one piece."

Upon our return to the abandoned airfield, we found my body right where we left it, sparkler still in hand. It still felt just as weird as it had a few hours prior, though, to see myself in the third person.

"Come to think of it," I said, "didn't you say there was some sort of time limit for how long we can interact? I feel like it was a *lot* shorter last time."

"It's because you were in soul form this time," said Ayane.

My body was my vessel—it bound me to the world of the living, and through it I was able to interact with society and the world around me. But if your goal was to commune with the souls of the dead, it was apparently only a hindrance.

I walked over to my vacant vessel and pressed a weightless palm against its back—and an instant later, I was back in my own skin. As gravity once again took its hold over me, I very nearly fell to my knees. Almost immediately, an aching fatigue shot through my head. My only guess was that, as part of the body-soul reuniting process, my physical brain was overheating from being forced to process the past few hours of stimuli all at once. I lifted my weary head and saw that Ayane's spectral form—that was so clear and vibrant to me just a moment ago—had grown hazy and indistinct. It was as though she could vanish into thin air at any moment.

"I had fun today," she said. "Thanks for hearing me out, Tomoya-kun."

And before I could even think of a suitable farewell, the wind picked up and took the Summer Ghost in its wake. As the tall grass once again began to sway and the insects resumed their songs, the sparkler fell from my fingertips onto the asphalt—and for a second time, I was left standing on the runway, alone with my thoughts once more.

Neither Aoi nor Ryo said a word as I recounted the events from the night before. By the time I finished, all of the ice in their glasses had melted from the white-hot rays of summer sun that poured in through the window.

Now that I was finally done speaking, Ryo reached into his bag and pulled out a handful of pill containers. He took one each of a variety of different capsules and tablets, downing them all in one go with a swig of water.

"So...they still haven't found the culprit, then?" asked Aoi.

"Nope," I said. "But Ayane-san says she doesn't care all that much about bringing him to justice. She doesn't really bear him any ill will, apparently. If anything, it seems like she mostly feels bad for leaving her mom behind with no real way of ever learning the truth. If you ask me, that might even be the main reason her soul can't find closure."

"So in other words," said Ryo, "you think that's why she's still stuck in limbo, just floating around town as a wandering spirit?"

It seemed a likely enough explanation for why a deceased person's soul might not be able to rest in peace—a lingering regret that kept them bound here to Earth. Ayane almost certainly regretted getting into an argument with her mother that night and running out of the house on a sour note that never she was never able to resolve. She hadn't told me that herself in any explicit terms, but when I recalled the deep sorrow I sensed in her eyes last night, it was the only explanation that made sense.

"So what do you want to do about it, Tomoya?" asked Ryo.

"Sorry?" I replied. "I'm not sure what you mean."

"I mean, why did you call us out here to tell us all of that? Sure, yeah, we know that the bit about the Summer Ghost being a woman who committed suicide was made up now, but what exactly does her being murdered have to do with *us*?"

"I mean, nothing, I guess. I just figured I'd debrief you guys on my encounter with her last night."

"You *sure* that's all this is about?"

I knew what Ryo was getting at. I hemmed and hawed for a moment.

"Well, to be completely honest, I guess I just wanted to hear your guys' takes on the whole situation," I admitted. "What do you two think? If we put our heads together, do you think we could find Ayane-san's body?"

Ryo clearly assumed that the conversation would eventually take this turn, so he seemed unfazed by this question. Aoi, on the other hand, was downright flabbergasted.

"What? You want us to go *dig up a body*?!" she cried. Her voice was so loud that other customers at nearby tables started casting suspicious glances.

"Pipe down, you idiot," Ryo whispered harshly, bonking her lightly on the head. "You're gonna make a scene."

"Sorry, I just wasn't expecting *that*, okay?!"

"Anyway," I said, pivoting, "the main reason Ayane-san gave up on finding her body is apparently because even if she found it, she wouldn't be able to dig it up herself. But with *our* help, we could even find a way to get her remains back home to her mother."

Ryo let out a heavy sigh and shook his head. "And *why* exactly would you wanna do that?" he asked. "It just seems like a huge pain in the ass to me."

"I know, and believe me, part of me is right there with you.

That's why I'm so conflicted about the idea and wanted to get your opinions."

After all, I had no obligation to go so far out of my way to try to do this for Ayane, especially when she neither asked nor expected me to.

"Well, I don't have much longer to live, dude. And I'd really prefer to spend the time I have left doing stuff *I* wanna do, no offense. Sorry if that makes me selfish."

And with that, Ryo stood up from the table and reached for his wallet.

"No, no, no," I said, holding out my hand to stop him. "I've got it."

Ryo gave a slight nod, then shambled his way back toward the entrance. Aoi and I just sat there and watched him go until the door closed behind him.

"Do you think maybe he resents us a little bit?" asked Aoi.

"*Resents* us?" I said. "Why would he?"

"I mean, you and I are making the *choice* to kill ourselves when we could just as easily go on living... But for Ryo, that's not an option. He's only doing this because the alternative will be more painful in the long run. He wants to go out on his own terms. ...From his perspective, we must seem like a couple of ungrateful little brats."

"I wouldn't worry about that so much, honestly. He wouldn't have joined the forums and started messaging with us if he really felt that way, I don't think. Anyway, what do you think about the idea of trying to find Ayane-san's body, Aoi?"

"I think it's a nice idea, but I guess I'm just not sure how realistic it is. It feels like there's no way we'll actually find it," she said doubtfully. "Don't get me wrong—I'm still really grateful to have met her, and I'd love to help her out. But it's not like she's asking us to do it either, is she? I mean, did she even so much as *insinuate* that she wanted your help finding her body?"

"Nope. Not at all."

"Yeah, then I think maybe we should just leave it be. It could be that she'd rather we not poke our noses into her business. Plus, it might even be kind of cruel, in a way."

"How so?" I asked.

"I mean, imagine having your daughter's corpse suddenly show up on your doorstep one day after three long years of holding out hope for a miracle. For all we know, it could totally destroy her mother's will to live. At least with the way things are now, she still has a glimmer of hope to cling on to, even if she'll never find closure. Who are we to decide whether or not she'll be happier knowing the truth, y'know?"

"So that's your take, huh... Okay. Fair enough."

My thoughts were sort of split down the middle in that regard too, admittedly. Would her mother appreciate finally having closure, no matter how painful it might be? Or would it be more merciful to let her go on living with the hope that her daughter might still come home one day?

"I take it though that *you* really want to go looking for her?" asked Aoi.

"I think I'm about fifty-fifty on it," I said. "But I'd like to help her, if I can."

"And where does that desire come from, do you think?"

I thought back to the previous night, to the way Ayane laid her hand on top of her mother's as the older woman read.

"I'm not sure, honestly," I said. "But I'm definitely not fishing for gratitude or anything like that."

"I see, I see. Well, let Detective Aoi spell it out for you, because I think I've cracked the case," said Aoi, with a giddiness in her eyes like a child who'd just been given a new toy. "I think *someone's* got a little crush on Ayane-san and is just looking for excuses to keep going to the airfield and meeting up with her!"

"Yeah, maybe so," I admitted.

"Wait… Seriously?!" Aoi recoiled.

I didn't know much about love or what it felt like. All I knew was that I had the time of my life flying around hand in hand with her last night. Come to think of it, it was the first time I ever had the chance to take a girl on a "date" to my favorite museum too. I didn't think much of it at the time, but maybe I really was starting to fall for her.

"You might be right, honestly," I said. "Maybe I really am just looking for excuses to continue going to see her."

"Man, this sucks..." Aoi huffed. "It's no fun when you just admit it like that. At least let me tease you about it a little bit first! Sheesh."

"Anyway, thanks for entertaining the idea, at least, Aoi. I really appreciate knowing where you guys stand."

"Hey, don't mention it."

And with that, the two of us settled the bill and made our way out of the diner as well. The hot air rising up off the sun-beaten asphalt distorted the view so much that it made the buildings across the street look like wavering mirages.

"Man, what a scorcher," I said. "You'd gotta have a death wish to willingly walk outside in this heat."

"No kidding," said Aoi. "We better make sure not to die of heat exhaustion before we even have the *chance* to commit suicide. That'd be a pretty lame way to go."

Through squinting eyes, we waved each other goodbye and went our separate ways.

I spent the remaining half of the month of August doing little else but maintaining the status quo—going to and from cram school each day and buying practice workbooks for entrance exams I had no intention of taking. The Common Test for University Admissions was held in mid-January, after all—and I'd long since decided I wanted to be dead before then.

It wasn't like I actually picked a date or anything, but the idea of killing myself sometime around the end of the year had been bouncing around in my head for a while now. I always liked the way the whole city transformed itself during Christmastime. It made everything feel a little bit warmer in spite of the cold. I figured killing myself on or slightly after Christmas itself would be most comfortable for me, so I let Ryo and Aoi know that I was tentatively planning to do it sometime during the week of the 24th through the 31st—right between Christmas Eve and New Year's Eve.

"Gotcha," Ryo wrote back. *"It obviously depends on my symptoms, but I'll be sure to swing by your funeral if I can make it. I'll bring a condolence offering and everything."*

"Yeah, I'll come see you one last time too, assuming I'm still alive," wrote Aoi.

To say that I wasn't afraid of dying in the slightest would've been a lie. Why, just the other day when Ayane let go of my hand and let me fall down through the earth, I screamed at the top of my lungs in fear—in fear of death. Given that, I wasn't entirely mentally prepared to take my own life just yet. I even asked myself if perhaps I was getting cold feet about the whole idea, but the answer there was a decisive no as well. In a sense, I was in my own state of limbo—stuck between not being ready to die and wanting nothing more.

While checking my smartphone during a break at cram school, I saw a news article about a high school girl who killed herself by jumping in front of a speeding train. For a moment, I wondered if perhaps Aoi had taken the initiative and was the first of us to actually follow through on our little pact, but upon reading the article more closely, I found that the story was apparently from a completely different part of the country, so it couldn't have been her. There were a few other suicide-related articles that caught my eye, though—one about a struggling single mother in poverty who killed her two infant children and then slit her own throat rather than let them all starve to death. Another was about a middle-aged businessman who wrote a confession of guilt for embezzling company funds before drenching his entire body in gasoline and lighting himself on fire in a public park in broad daylight. Then, there was yet another about a town hall worker in her twenties who suffered ceaseless harassment from a superior. She drove to said superior's house in the middle of the night, lit a large amount of charcoal in her car, and died of carbon monoxide poisoning while parked in their driveway. This was a sobering reminder of just how many people there were in the world who wanted to kill themselves and just how many different ways there were to do it.

Though I had to admit, the story of the single mother who took her children with her *did* make me unreasonably angry. While she was almost certainly suffering and wasn't in a sound state of mind, you couldn't just take innocent children with no agency along with you to the grave. If you wanted to commit suicide, you had to do it alone—while also making sure to cause as little trouble for those around you as possible. It was practically an unwritten rule.

There were studies that suggested a majority of people who committed (or at least considered) suicide were people who somehow fell into a one-track mindset where—be it due to depression or some other mental disorder—they ultimately became convinced that death was the only answer to their problems. I wondered if this was the case for me as well. I didn't *think* it was, but then again, people with extremely narrow mindsets and cyclical thought processes didn't tend to be the most self-aware.

As evening fell, I left my cram school and headed for home. On my way to the station, I passed by an art supply store I used to frequent quite a bit during my junior high days—virtually every day, in fact. A group of college-aged kids emerged from the store just as I walked past the entrance, and they started walking down the sidewalk in the opposite direction. I could tell from their clothing and general vibes that they were probably art school students. They seemed to be having an awful lot of fun chatting about whatever it was they were discussing. As I turned and watched them walk down the street for a moment, a twinge of pain shot through my chest.

Then, as if the universe truly did have a sense of irony, a car I knew all too well pulled up along the sidewalk almost immediately thereafter. My mother rolled the window down and leaned her head out.

"Tomoya."

"Mother."

"I had a feeling you'd be getting out of class right about now, so I figured I'd swing by," she said. "Get in."

I walked over and climbed into the passenger seat. My mother waited for me to buckle my seatbelt and then promptly took off. She always drove to work and would occasionally pick me up from cram school on her way home when the timing worked out. I appreciated it a lot, actually.

My mother was a safe but decisive driver. While half-listening to the news program playing on the radio, I gazed lazily out the window. There was a group of high school kids hanging out in the parking lot of the corner store—both boys and girls. They looked like they just got back from a trip to the beach or the amusement park and were really laughing it up.

My mother cast them a sidelong glance. "Well, they certainly seem to be enjoying frittering away their little summer vacations," she said. "You'd better take care not to end up like them, Tomoya. They'll never amount to anything in life."

My mother always did that—she'd lambast "problem children" she saw as potential bad influences on me with a slew of scathing denouncements. In her mind, kids like them would only ever grow up to be disappointments to their parents, would never get into a halfway decent college, and would struggle to find any employer who'd take them. She genuinely seemed to believe this too—and while I didn't think the simple act of hanging out with one's friends was such a horrible thing, I really didn't have the energy to fight her on it at that moment. All I could really do was nod and say, "Yeah, no kidding."

We pulled further away from the commercial district that surrounded the station toward our more residential part of town. The newscaster on the radio was giving a report on some international border dispute happening overseas—a lot of innocent civilians had just been killed by a suicide bomber. It was the fault of religious extremists, apparently—so extreme that they would gladly lay down their lives and take countless others with them for the sake of their so-called faith, all while truly believing they were completely in the right and dying for a righteous cause.

"How are your studies coming along?" my mother asked. "Remind me how far you are in math again?"

"Right now, I'm doing binomial coefficients, graphing all possible paths of a given parabolic equation through the coordinate plane... Stuff like that," I said.

She liked to ask me questions about each of the subjects I was learning in cram school—and if ever she found something for which my understanding appeared to be lacking in her view, she'd let out a sigh of disappointment and chide me as she drove.

"Why can't you just stay on top of things, like I did at your age?" she said.

As her lecture went on, I could feel my heart beginning to deflate in my chest. I slouched my shoulders shamefully at the implication that I was defective in some way. Even though I knew I was well above average for my grade, I could never be proud of that fact. I would never be enough for her, and that had been instilled in me from an early age.

"Have you settled on your first-choice college yet?" she asked.

"Yeah," I said.

I'd written the names of both my first choice and a few alternates down on my ideal higher education plan report that I was expected to turn in to my homeroom teacher at the start of fall semester. Not that there was much point in doing so other than saving face, though—I would be dead and buried by the time exam season rolled around.

"You're very blessed, you know that?" said my mother. "Do you have any idea how expensive it is to send your child off to college? When I was your age, my family's finances couldn't pay for my education. I had to work multiple jobs while in school just to pay for my own tuition. You've got it easy, I tell you. I worked awfully hard to save up money for your college fund, all to ensure you'll be successful in life."

As we made our way down the residential streets, I found it gradually getting harder and harder to breathe. I wondered if the suffocating feeling I was having right now was anything like the literal suffocation that Ayane suffered, being buried under the dirt in that suitcase. Anytime I was trapped in a room or an enclosed space like this and forced to listen to my mother speaking at me, it was practically torture.

I wanted nothing more than to open the passenger side door and jump out onto the pavement and make a run for it. How freeing would that be? I might even have done it too, if it weren't for my inner sense of reason telling me that would only make things worse in the long run. Thankfully, my thought processes hadn't become *that* cyclical and blinkered, not yet.

I did still feel, however, that death would be a relief—even if I would be committing sacrilege in my father's eyes. After all, his religion forbade suicide for any reason as it was essentially murder of the self. Only God was allowed to give or take life; it was a grave sin for a human to do the same. My life belonged to God, and I was forbidden from taking a life, even from myself. To commit suicide was to commit an act of betrayal against God, and the punishment after death would be the revocation of my eternal rest.

But *I* had no religion, so these taboos didn't intimidate me one bit. I only felt bad about it because it would make me a disappointment to my father. Perhaps the gift of life had been given to me by some all-powerful god—but it belonged to me now. It was no one else's but mine—both to live, and to take.

"I brought you into this world," said my mother, "so it falls to me to make sure you find and stick to the right track through life."

She was always trying to take the initiative in my life on my behalf. *She* was the one who always decided where I would go next, just like how *she* was the one who picked out all the "acceptable" colleges for me to choose from. By this point, I had completely lost the will to fight her on it—and perhaps that was why I was so dead set committing suicide. Maybe that would finally show her that my life hadn't been hers to do with as she saw fit. Maybe then she'd see that the choice was really mine in the end.

"I wonder if maybe I'm just too weak to go on living like everyone else seems to do," Aoi wrote, in a paragraph she posted

to our group DM. *"Like, I'm always stressing myself out over the tiniest things that I know other people wouldn't even give a second thought. I'll get excited and say something that's maybe a little too excited in the heat of the moment. Later on, I regret it later and wish I was dead."*

She didn't seem to be looking for a response to what she was saying, or like she wanted any sort of advice—this was just her own way of venting.

"At least death is quick. You just have to endure a few moments of pain and then you can sleep forever. I'm still not sure how I should do it, honestly—I did a little research into hydrogen sulfide the other day but I'm not sure if that's realistic for me or not."

"Wouldn't if I were you. Apparently the lasting side effects are pretty brutal if you screw that one up and somehow survive."

"Yeah. And wasn't there that one story about the guy whose family tried to save him and ended up breathing in too much of it themselves? Bad idea, for sure."

We talked about different suicide methods like this from time to time.

"Remind me again, Aoi—didn't you say you were gonna decide when to kill yourself based on the weather that day?"

"Yeah. I wanna wake up that morning, open the curtains, and if I see a beautiful blue sky out the window? I'll go, 'Yeah, maybe today's the day.' So I'm thinking something quick and

easy that I can set up on whim whenever the impulse strikes me would be good. Maybe just plain old hanging or something would be my best bet."

"What about sleeping pills? Just gotta swallow 'em, and you're good to go."

"I dunno about that. You've gotta take a heck of a lot of those to actually overdose."

"Plus, wouldn't it be kinda weird to wake up the morning of, see that it's a beautiful day, and then go right back to sleep?"

"Not if you ask me. It'd be just like going back to bed and sleeping in for a little while."

"Yeah, or for an eternity."

I messaged back and forth with them like this pretty frequently these days—on the train to and from cram school, and during breaks between study hours. Aoi apparently spent her entire summer vacation cooped up at home. As for Ryo, on days when he didn't have to go to the hospital, he said he often went and sat in on his underclassmen's basketball practices or spent quality time with his family.

"Come to think of it, I read that there's a way to hang yourself while lying in bed. Seems kind of counterintuitive to me."

"Nah. As long as there's something to hang the rope from above your neck, you can totally do it. People hang themselves in their hospital beds all the time, apparently."

"Is that something you're considering, Ryo-kun?"

"If my health deteriorates to the point where I'm totally bedridden, maybe, yeah. But I'd much rather pick something else before it ever gets that bad. Rather not have to watch myself turn into a total *invalid if I have the choice."*

I could understand that—especially for a once-promising athlete like Ryo.

"It's not like I have much longer to live regardless, so yeah, I'd at least like to die before I lose my dignity. There's no chance of me winning against this thing, so I'd rather just withdraw from the match. Find someplace high up with a nice view to jump off of while my legs still work and let gravity do the rest."

Only ten days of summer vacation now remained; before long, it would be fall. I wondered how much longer it would even be *possible* to go and see Ayane, assuming the rumors about her only appearing during the summer were true. Once autumn fell, it was entirely likely that no number of sparklers would be able to call her spirit forth again—at least not until next summer. However, I supposed it was equally likely that no one had ever *tried* going there and lighting sparklers at night during any other time of year, given that summer was the generally agreed-upon fireworks season.

But when, specifically, did summer turn to fall? At least here in Japan, we defined summer as the three-month period of June, July, and August, although the Japan Meteorological

Agency considered any day on which the peak temperature rose above twenty-five degrees Celsius to be part of the "summer season." Perhaps I could still meet with Ayane in September as well, as long as the weather stayed warm.

"So, hey, what's the latest with Ayane-san's body?" asked Aoi. *"Have you been looking for it or what?"*

"No," I wrote back. *"Been way too busy with cram school."*

If I truly couldn't see her again after summer came to an end, and if I really did intend to kill myself by the end of the year, then now might be my only chance to go and find her remains. And if I didn't step up to the plate, she could very well remain a missing person forever—a spirit with one lingering regret in her heart, doomed to haunt this city for eternity. I asked myself again: Was I going to do this, or not?

One day in the last week of August, I came home from cram school to find that my sketchbook—which had been stashed away among my heavy winter clothes in my closet like usual—was lying front and center on the living room table. It took my brain a few moments to register what was happening and I simply stood there in the center of the room, stock still and dumbfounded.

"Sit down, Tomoya."

This voice belonged to my mother, who was just now walking in from the study. She pounded the tabletop with her palms, giving me the same look of disapproval she gave to badly behaved children in public. I could feel my stomach shriveling up into a ball.

"You've been drawing again, I see," she continued, staring me down from the opposite side of the living room table.

"In between study sessions, yeah," I said. "It's like a palate cleanser. Helps keep my mind refreshed and engaged."

"Then why were you hiding it from me?"

"Because I figured you'd throw it in the garbage if you found out," I said. "Why were *you* rummaging through my closet?"

"Don't start with me. *I'm* the one paying the bills here. Once you start pulling your own weight, maybe *then* we can have a little chat about privacy."

My mother then proceeded to flip silently through my sketchbook, page by page. The room was so quiet that I could hear the wall clock ticking out each and every excruciating second. The sound of her methodically turning over each page of thick sketch paper was almost unbearably loud as well.

"Did we not agree that you were going to stop with all of this art nonsense in order to fully devote yourself to your schoolwork?" she asked.

"I already told you," I said. "It's just to help me relax a little between study sessions."

"I'm very worried about you, Tomoya. I don't want you getting obsessed with these silly little doodles of yours again, like you were back in junior high."

I already knew, of course, that this was all my artistic achievements back then had ever amounted to in her mind—nothing more than silly little doodles.

"I'm not saying there's no value in drawing whatsoever, of course," she went on. "I think it's a very healthy way to cultivate a sense of aesthetics in early childhood. But unless you're an absolute prodigy, you should *not* be wasting this much time playing with crayons and colored pencils after elementary school. Do you have *an*y idea how embarrassed I was to see you still drawing like this in junior high? Why, I'm *mortified* to know you've been doing it even in *high school*."

My mother set the sketchbook back down on the table—opened to a page featuring a full-body sketch of Ayane with her feet floating ever so slightly off the ground. I liked this drawing an awful lot; I thought it captured her ineffable, otherworldly aura quite well for a mere pencil sketch. The viewer could instantly tell that it depicted a supernatural being descending from the skies, just about to set her feet down on solid earth.

"Okay," I said, hoping to placate her. "You win. I'll stop."

"Oh really, now? And how do I know you're not just saying that to end this conversation faster?" she asked.

"What can I do to make you believe me?"

Silence. I waited on pins and needles for my mother to respond. After a few moments' pause, she reached down, picked up my sketchbook, and held it out to me.

"Dispose of it," she said. "Tear out every page, one by one, and then rip them up and throw them in the garbage. If you can do that, then I suppose I'll believe you."

I took the sketchbook from her but hesitated. I knew, of course, that drawing my mother's ire at this venture would be a very bad idea and that it would serve me best to just do as I was told and get rid of it. I could always buy another sketchbook and continue drawing in secrecy, after all. I had zero intention of actually quitting—but I had no problem with paying her lip service to make her believe that I was.

Even so, I was awfully fond of several of the drawings I'd done in this particular sketchbook. The one of Ryo, Aoi, and me walking to the abandoned airfield that day. And the ones of Ayane and I walking through the museum at night, and of us sitting on the radio tower together. The idea of simply disposing of these fond memories did not sit well with me.

"What's the matter?" my mother asked. "Can't do it?"

I looked down at the full-body sketch of Ayane, floating in midair. I hadn't made any copies of the drawing or even taken a picture of it with my phone. All I could really do now was try my damnedest to singe its memory into my retinas.

Ever since I was a little boy, whenever my mother and I had confrontations like this, I often felt as though I was having an out-of-body experience, like I was hanging from the ceiling, looking down at my body in the third person. I would simply turn off my emotions and quash all of my willpower and volition as an individual to become little more than a puppet that nodded along and agreed to do my mother's bidding. I knew now, of course, that there was a name for this mental phenomenon: dissociation.

I grabbed the top edge of the page with both hands, and by pulling each side in opposite directions, I ripped my drawing of Ayane right down the middle. I then tore the remaining half out. My mother seemed satisfied with this, so I continued ripping the halves up into even smaller pieces. Once that was done, I got to work trashing all of the other pages as well, shredding each one with my own two hands until eventually, all that remained of my sketchbook was a pile of paper scraps.

"A wise decision," said my mother. "You don't have the talent to make art for a living, so if you want to grow up to be an adult that can support yourself, you'd do well to invest that time and energy into your studies instead. Now then—let's eat, shall we?"

My mother smiled, then walked over into the kitchen to get started on dinner. I gathered up all the torn scraps of paper with both hands, then walked over and threw them in the garbage.

Had I been a bit younger, I might have cried at being forced to destroy my own creations like this. Had I been a slightly less pathetic human, I might have fought my mother on it, and continued arguing with her until I somehow won myself the right to continue drawing. But I was neither of those things, and having lived alone with her like this for so many years now, I simply accepted this relationship dynamic as the static quo. I knew that at this point, it was entirely futile to stand up for myself, and I could no longer summon forth the willpower to even try. All I could really do was continue playing my role as her dutiful honor student—because we both knew full well that I was too weak to do anything else.

I remained in this dissociated state for quite some time after that, with my mind all but divorced from my corporeal self—though as far as out-of-body experiences went, it was nothing at all like the thrilling night I'd shared with Ayane a couple weeks prior.

Late that night, after ensuring that my mother was fast asleep, I snuck out of the apartment, being careful not to make a sound as I slipped my shoes on my feet in the entryway. Upon exiting the building, I was met by a humid breeze that shook the leaves in the trees lining the road. I walked down the sidewalk beneath the endless streetlights with no destination in mind. I just needed the taste of fresh air in my lungs again. I'd been fighting back a torrent of emotions from being forced to rip up my own artwork all night, and I couldn't hold it in any longer.

I stopped for a moment and peered down into the small stream that flowed alongside the promenade—but all I could see reflected in its waters was a shadowy silhouette of myself, backlit by the lamplight shining down from above.

If I died here tonight, would I be freed from all of this? Would I finally be able to feel at peace?

I was struck by a sudden urge—I wanted to see Ayane. I recalled the night we flew together as ghosts through the skies. I was free that evening—free to leave my fleshy prison behind and soar away from the world and all its troubles. If I could die and become a ghost like her, I'd never have to feel this pain, this *suffocation*, ever again. And if so, why *wouldn't* I want to die right here and now? I knew I probably couldn't drown myself here in this shallow stream—but I knew that if I followed it long enough, it emptied out into a much wider river. I could easily find someplace deep enough to do the deed.

But then again...Ayane was still suffering from regret, even in death. I could see in her eyes, when she looked down upon her mother, that she hadn't truly been released from the pain of living. Not yet, anyway. In that case, maybe I wouldn't find the relief I sought in death either. Perhaps I'd still feel suffocated by these inescapable thoughts, even as a soul freed from material shackles and confinement. I assumed Ayane's ghost would wander these streets for eternity, never able to let go of those lingering regrets, and especially once her mother died without ever learning the truth.

I could die just about anytime I wanted. I didn't *have* to wait until the end of the year if I really couldn't take it any longer. But before I did, I at least wanted to try talking to Ayane one last time. Such were my thoughts as I strolled aimlessly down the sidewalk.

I wondered how she really felt about the notion that her body was buried somewhere in a suitcase beneath the dirt, probably rotted to the bone by now. Was she really okay with just giving up the search and leaving it be? Or was she still holding out hope, somewhere deep down, that someone would come along and dig her up one day? If that was truly her last remaining desire, then I alone was uniquely positioned to help her achieve it.

I could deal with another couple weeks of suffocation if it meant putting an end to hers. And right now, all I wanted to do, more than anything in the world, was to find that suitcase, open it up, and give Ayane her first taste of fresh air in so, so long.

Five

Summer Ghost

NOW, ONLY FIVE DAYS remained of my summer vacation. On my way home from cram school, I decided to make a little detour. I bought some fireworks, took the train to the bus stop, and by the time I arrived at the abandoned airfield, the sun had already set. The sky's brightness had left for the day and had turned a deep shape of blue. The summer constellations shone down on the runway on me where I stood—sparkler in one hand, lighter in the other.

Once I ignited the sparkler, the tip quickly swelled up into that familiar molten drop, and sparks began to fly.

As humans, we instinctively associated the dark of night with death. Our lives were just a flicker in the dark, after all—a tiny light that would surely fade soon enough, but we prayed would continue to shine with each passing breath. Perhaps that was why we found fireworks so compelling, so innately beautiful.

Before long, the sparkling grew fiercer, and the voices of the insects went silent. I could feel the flow of time slowing to a crawl once more. I could tell that she would be here before long, and sure enough, just as I thought that, she called my name.

"Fancy seeing you here, Tomoya-kun."

I didn't know exactly how long she was standing there in front of me—but the way she was doing so made it feel like she had been there all along and I simply couldn't see her before. I let go of my sparkler, knowing full well that it would remain suspended in midair for as long as time was stopped.

"You're looking as ready to die as always, I see," she observed, sounding almost disappointed in me.

"Glad to see you're looking well, Ayane-san," I said, shrugging it off.

"Pretty poor choice of words to describe a dead person, don't you think?"

"It's just a casual greeting," I said back. "No need to fixate on it."

As always, there was an air of fragile ephemerality about her—like a gentle breeze could make her vanish like mist in the wind. Like she was a mirage, almost, because even though I could see her right here in front of me, it felt as if she were actually somewhere far, far away.

"So, what brings you here this evening?" she asked me.

"Well, I've been doing a lot of thinking," I replied. "And I've got a proposition for you that I think you might be interested in."

"Oh really?"

"Ever heard of *The Legend of Sleepy Hollow*, Ayane-san?"

"Is that the one with the headless horseman?" she asked.

"You got it."

It was an old American fairy tale that had seen several adaptations over the past couple of centuries. It was about a haunted forest glen by the name of Sleepy Hollow, and the ghost of a decapitated soldier on horseback was said to roam there.

"I think I saw a movie based on it once."

"You remember how the horseman's riding around for eternity in search of his severed head, then, I take it?" I asked.

"Yeah," Ayane said. "What about it?"

"Well, I was just thinking that sounds an awful lot like your situation, is all."

"So, what—you think I'm gonna be roaming around this city for eternity in search of my lost body?"

"I don't know. Are you?" I asked.

"I mean, I definitely was at first. But like I told you last time, I gave up the search. Because even if I found it, it's not like I could do anything about it."

"Maybe *you* couldn't. But I certainly could—as your one ally who's teetering right on the border between life and death."

Perhaps the whole reason she started appearing before people as the so-called Summer Ghost was because she was waiting for someone to come along who could help her find her body. Someone not yet incorporeal who might listen to her plight.

"We can have you remove my soul from my body again, like you did last time, and then go searching underground," I continued. "Once we find the suitcase, I can go back into my body and alert the police to its location. Or I can go there and dig it up myself if I have to."

"You'd do that for me, Tomoya-kun?" she asked.

"I mean, unless you rather I stayed out of it, that is."

"No, no! I'd be so grateful, actually."

This came as a relief to hear; ever since Aoi and Ryo pointed out that there was a good chance she wasn't looking for any help finding her body, I was a little concerned that perhaps I'd be overstepping some boundaries with this little proposal.

"But why would you go to all that trouble for my sake?" asked Ayane. "It's not like there's anything in it for you."

"Just killing time until I die, really. But I guess that's all life is in general, isn't it?"

"Y'know, for a high school kid, you're quite the little smart aleck," she said. Then, her expression took a serious shift, and she extended her right hand out to me. Her slender arm almost looked painted, impressionist, with its ghostly form threatening to melt into the background at any moment. "Well, thank you, Tomoya-kun. So...when would you like to get started?"

"Right now, if possible. Gotta make sure we find it before summer ends."

And with that, we shook on it. The moment her fingers touched mine, my field of vision went out of alignment—I assumed this meant my soul was now dislodged from my body. Ayane took me by the hand and pulled me all the way out, dragging me up along with her into the sky. She turned and looked back at me as we rose higher and higher into the ether—and the look on her face was one of genuine exhilaration. I was so glad I mustered up the courage to suggest doing this.

Leaving my body behind on the ground, we soared through the abandoned outskirts and went back toward the residential part of town where streetlamps and window lights spread out before us like glimmers of gold.

Really, though—where could her body be buried? I tried to think if there was any way we could narrow down our search area a bit. There were railway tracks running back and forth like stitches, sewing one neighborhood together with the next. Lines from several different rail companies passed through this area, and she and I looked down at the tracks.

"Do you remember hearing any trains while you were being buried?" I asked.

"Actually, yes," she said. "They were pretty loud, in fact. Even through the suitcase."

"What kind of sound did it make? Any characteristic motor sounds or anything that stuck in your mind?"

"No, not particularly… It just sounded like a regular train to me. Maybe if I were a train fanatic, I'd be able to tell you more and we could narrow our options down a bit, but I'm not, sadly. All I remember is the vague sound of trains passing by."

"Did you hear any railway crossing bells?"

"Well… Now that you mention it, I guess I didn't."

In that case, we could probably cross any areas with a railway crossing nearby off our search list.

"How long could you hear each passing train for, do you recall?" I asked.

"I really don't at this point, but I want to say it was more than five seconds, at least? Maybe even closer to ten?"

"They must've been going pretty fast, then."

"Yeah, it definitely didn't seem like they were slowing down to pull into a station or anything—just speeding right on by."

That meant we could presumably remove anywhere especially close to a station from the list as well. It would make sense to focus our search near long straightaways with few crossings where trains were free to go at full speed. Additionally, the fact that she thought it may have even been audible for a full ten seconds seemed to suggest that these were likely not just one- or two-car trains, but fairly long ones.

"I guess it's possible that they buried you in a ditch on some unused plot of land adjacent to the railroad," I posited.

"Yeah, or maybe the driver just lived near the train tracks and buried me on his own property," said Ayane. "Believe me, I've done my fair share of searching too—and I had the same thought as you. Went around indiscriminately checking underground in the backyards of houses along the railways, but to no avail. There are just too many different places to look, so I gave up."

This was a fair point—Japan was littered from top to bottom with rail lines. It would be preposterous to suggest that we check the immediate vicinity of each and every one. But we should've been able to narrow down the search area at least a *little* bit more as we knew the killer could have only driven so far from Ayane's neighborhood with her in his trunk...though exactly *how* far depended entirely on just how long she was passed out after the initial impact and before regaining consciousness. If it was only ten short minutes or so, then we could establish a pretty solid search radius from the scene of the accident.

"I know this is a huge shot in the dark," I said, "but do you have any idea how long you were out, by chance?"

"I really don't, unfortunately," said Ayane.

"Do you recall if the blood from your injury already dried?"

"No idea."

"Well, do you at least remember approximately what time you had that argument with your mother and ran out of the house?" I asked.

"Around 9:30 at night, I think. God, that was so stupid of me..."

She cast her gaze down to the ground; her regret was palpable. After all, had it not been for that fight, she would most likely still be alive today.

"And how much time passed between you leaving your house and you getting hit by that car? Any idea?" I asked.

"About fifteen minutes, maybe," she said.

This would mean that she'd been run over sometime around 9:45 p.m. In which case, it seemed unlikely that she would've been unconscious for several hours as the trains only ran until about midnight in this area. It also seemed like she was hearing them periodically, so it couldn't have been only the very last train either. Additionally, unless the driver had a giant travel suitcase in his trunk for whatever reason, it would have taken him some time to procure one and shove her body inside. That would have taken more time, obviously, which meant that at the very most, he could have only driven about two hours from the scene of the crime—barring the possibility that she had been unconscious all night, of course. If she had, and the trains she was hearing were actually from sometime the next day, then we'd have to dramatically expand our search area...so I prayed that hadn't been the case. In any case, your average unintentional murderer would likely be in a frantic state of mind and would simply want to get the suitcase buried under the cover of night. They would not want to risk being seen in the morning light, especially if they didn't have a disposal plan thought out well in advance.

After getting the approximate address from Ayane, I drew a map of the surrounding area in my head. It was awfully inconvenient that I couldn't just plug the coordinates into a smartphone app while in soul form. But in any event, I mentally mapped out a rough circle around the scene of the accident and picked out a few initial candidates for places to search in that area that were near train lines. In general, I picked out straightaways for longer multi-car trains with no railroad crossings nearby that were within a two-hour drive of the scene. That narrowed things down quite a bit, but there were still a huge number of places to check—and with no other leads, we had little choice but to search them all one by one.

We flew through the night sky over to Ayane's neighborhood and began our search there, moving outward. We descended to the railroad tracks and let our bodies sink beneath the gravel-covered earth. There was no physical resistance to stop us while in soul form, of course, so it hardly felt any different from being submerged in a deep body of water.

"This is just a hunch," I said, "but I'm pretty sure he couldn't have buried you all that far underground either."

"True," said Ayane. "If he dug the hole himself with only a shovel, he couldn't have made it more than a meter or so deep."

Just to be sure, I asked if she happened to hear anything that sounded like heavy machinery at the time, but she said no. So, we only really had to look as deep underground as, say, your average public pool. This was helpful as, like before, our vision was fairly obscured and indistinct while underground. We could tell where nearby manmade structures and building foundations were, for instance, but couldn't clearly make out anything beyond our immediate vicinity. It really did feel like swimming through a lake full of murky water.

We looked around under the ground for what felt like two hours, diving into gardens and ditches and abandoned lots and farmlands straddling the railroad where someone could have feasibly buried a suitcase. Occasionally, while zooming our way through the ground, one of us would end up lost in an underground parking garage, or in the basement of some random person's house. In those cases, we would head back above ground, call out to the other person, and regroup to regain our bearings.

But there were no suitcases to be found anywhere we looked. Although searching in soul form like this took no toll on our stamina, after a while, Ayane suggested we call it quits for the night.

"How come?" I asked. "I'm good to keep going if you are."

"It's not that," she said. "Our worlds can't stay overlapped for much longer. We have to get you back in your own skin before they pull apart."

"And what happens if we don't?"

The most obvious possibility, I supposed, was that if my soul remained here in limbo with Ayane's, my body would just drop dead where we left it on the runway once time started moving forward again. As someone who was planning to kill themselves anyway, the thought didn't disturb me all that much. The only problem would be that we'd no longer have a way of letting anyone in the world of the living know where the suitcase was in the event that we found it.

"I don't think anything will *happen*, per se," said Ayane. "At least that's what my intuition tells me, anyway—the same way it told me that if I touched you, I could pluck your soul right out of your body. It's just instinctive ghost knowledge, I guess. Something tells me that even if we don't take you back, you'll just wake back at the airfield in your own body when the time comes anyway."

"Want to give it a try, just to see?" I asked, half-jokingly, but well aware that if her instincts turned out to be wrong, it could mean my death.

But instead, we headed back to the abandoned airfield, making small talk as we flew.

"If we want to have any hope of finding your body before summer ends, then I guess we can't afford to take things slow. We'll have to continue the search every night from here on out."

While there was certainly some ambiguity in terms of when exactly summer ended and autumn began, there was no denying that we had precious few days remaining before Ayane could no longer appear—which, according to her, was indeed an *actual* phenomenon and not just a part of the urban legend.

"Yeah, no," she said. "Once autumn rolls around, I won't be able to see you again until summertime next year."

"Do you know why that is, exactly?" I asked.

"I guess I just figure it's because Obon happens during the summer."

"I didn't realize you were Buddhist, Ayane-san."

Though deeply rooted in the ancient Japanese belief of ancestral spirits as well, there could be no denying that Obon was primarily a Buddhist festival.

"I'm not," she clarified. "But everyone knows summer's the season of supernatural stuff, right? That's when they play all those ghost stories and whatnot on TV after all. Not that I would ever watch any of them myself—I'm way too afraid of ghosts."

"Beg your pardon?"

"What?" she asked.

"...Never mind. But yes, apparently the whole 'summer is a time for ghost stories' thing does trace its roots back to Obon, originally."

According to one famed scholar of Japanese folklore, the custom originated in the traditional kyogen plays based around ceremonies for the repose of departed souls that rural communities would perform during Obon. The art of kabuki theater would eventually adopt these customs into many now-iconic plays—perhaps the most famous of which being the *Tokaido Yotsuya Kaidan*—and it was from these performances that the notion of ghost stories having a "chilling" effect that helped to stave off the brutal midsummer heat was born.

"That's awfully culture-specific though," I noted. "Like, if you were born in Mexico, for example, I wonder if you'd instead only be visible during the fall?"

"Sorry, I'm not seeing the connection here," replied Ayane.

"Well, because they celebrate *their* 'Day of the Dead' in November."

The famous Dia de los Muertos, known for its iconic painted skeletons, was a day of celebration for the departed. The West, in turn, had long observed a similar custom in All Hallows' Eve on almost the exact same day—though this was originally more a time of reverence compared to the festive holiday it had now become. But as a result of these traditional observances, late fall had become for the West what summer was for Japan: a time to honor the spirits of the dead, and a time for scary stories in turn.

Ayane seemed impressed by this trivia. "You know, Tomoya-kun—for a high school kid, you certainly know your stuff," she said.

And almost immediately thereafter, my vision blacked out.

Gravity regained its hold on my legs, and I fell to my knees on the asphalt, back in my body once more. A warm summer night's breeze blew through the airfield, and the tall grass lining the runway began to stir. My sparkler lay extinguished on the ground before me, but the smell of burning gunpowder still hung in the air.

The ghost of Sato Ayane was now nowhere to be seen.

We were still quite a way away from the airfield when my soul instantly snapped back into my body—presumably because time had run out, just as Ayane described. I assumed this was a testament as to just how tightly bound the soul was to the body under normal circumstances—though it could also be that physical distance held no bearing over how quickly the two could be reunited.

I wondered, if I were to continue lighting sparklers one after another, if I could meet up with her again and continue our search for the suitcase all night until I ran out. But within seconds of being back in my own body, my head started ringing and I felt an intense sense of fatigue. The same thing happened last time—and back then, I assumed it was a result of my brain being forced to instantly process all of the stimuli and memories I experienced in soul form over the previous several hours. It was dizzying.

"Well..." I whispered to no one. "See you tomorrow, then."

I could only hope, as I rose to my feet, that these words would somehow reach her, wherever she was. I let myself back out of the area via the hole in the rusty chain-link fence and headed for home.

The following night, I returned to the airfield as promised. The usual ritual ensued: the sparkler burned bright for a moment, and then the wind stopped, and all grew silent. The Summer Ghost revealed herself, emerging from between the tall blades of grass.

Ayane looked around, examining each of our faces one by one in the moonlight. "I see you've brought company today," she said. "Evening, Aoi-chan, Ryo-kun."

"Yeah, long time no see," replied Aoi. She had been crouched down on the runway, gazing into her sparkler, but now she rose to her feet and smiled.

Ryo pulled his hands out of his pockets and bowed his head politely. "Tomoya got in touch, so we came along to help out," he said.

"Just figured a team of four can cover more ground than a team of two," I said.

Though we narrowed our search radius quite a bit, it didn't change the fact that we were still underground, more or less groping through the dark. We needed all the help we could get—which is why I reached out to Aoi and Ryo via DM last night and let them know that Ayane was fully on board with the idea of us helping to find her body, assuming they didn't mind helping. The two of them weren't especially enthusiastic about the idea when I first brought it up back at the diner, so I was a little worried they might've said no. But as soon as I told them it was what Ayane herself wanted, they immediately changed their tunes and said they'd be happy to join the search.

"Well, thank you all," said Ayane, her tone apologetic. "I wish I could do something to return the favor."

"Don't sweat it," said Ryo. "As far as I'm concerned, I already owe you big-time, anyhow."

"Really? What did I ever do for you, Ryo-kun?"

"You set my worst fears at ease," he said. "Now I know that death ain't the end after all."

"Yeah, I'm really grateful to have had the chance to meet you too, Ayane-san," said Aoi. "So I wanted to do *something* to repay you, if I could. Besides, it's not like I'd be doing anything more productive with my time otherwise—I'd just be staying home and playing video games, probably. Figured I might as well get out there and make some nice memories, given that this might be my last summer and all."

"Yeah, right," Ryo teased. "I bet you just didn't wanna feel left out."

"Nuh-uh! Hey! Why are you bullying me all of a sudden?!" Aoi whined.

"It was just a joke, my friend. Chill."

And so without further ado, we prepared to begin the night's search—starting, of course, with Ayane removing each of our souls from our bodies. I was already used to the phenomenon by this point, but Ryo and Aoi seemed particularly unnerved by it. Aoi squealed and fell backward, flapping her arms and legs wildly to try to regain her balance—but her feet only slipped right through the ground.

"Just calm down, Aoi-chan," said Ayane. "You have to straighten out your mind and stand with your heart—not your legs."

Now that the two girls were both in ghost form and able

to actually touch one another, Ayane helped Aoi back up to her feet. Aoi then proceeded to cling to Ayane's arm, like she was trying to hold on for dear life.

"I don't know about this, Ayane-san!" she cried out. "Maybe I'm not cut out for flying after all!"

Ryo, meanwhile, had gotten the hang of it right away. He was having a ball flying freely through the air.

"Damn, you could do some totally badass dunks like this!" He then proceeded to demonstrate via pantomime before deftly touching back down to the earth.

And so the four of us set off, flying through the night sky toward the area where Ayane and I had started looking for the suitcase yesterday. I already explained the search criteria to the newcomers, so they knew what to look for. After crossing over the floodplain, we gazed down at the city lights and headed for the railroad tracks. Aoi was still struggling to find her groove with the whole flying thing, so Ayane was dragging her along by the hand. If she didn't, Aoi'd only start tumbling down to the ground like I had my first time. But even so, she seemed downright awestruck by the sheer beauty of it all—gazing down upon our familiar nightscape from high in the sky.

"Let's try looking around here tonight," I suggested, and we all headed down to a lightly wooded area slightly removed from the residential districts. There, the only things straddling the train tracks were untouched thickets and a few lumber yards.

"Yeah, if I were trying to hide a body, this is prolly the sort of place I'd wanna do it. No houses nearby, which means no eyewitnesses in the dead of night," commented Ryo, taking a quick look around the area before promptly heading down to check underground. He dove down between the rails and the crossties and disappeared beneath the gravel.

"Here, Aoi-chan," said Ayane. "Take my hand and we'll go together."

"Yes, please," said a still very skittish Aoi.

"If anyone finds anything that looks promising, just shout it out."

Even underground, with no air through which sound waves could travel, our voices could reach each other just fine. Communicating in ghost form seemed to work through an entirely different mechanism than the physics involved in normal speech.

We swam through the ground in search of the suitcase, being careful never to delve deeper than about one meter below the surface. Unfortunately, all we really found were bits of rubble and the occasional piece of furniture or household appliances that someone had seen fit to illegally dump in the woods. At one point, we did happen upon a rectangular box that looked as though a human might fit inside—but upon closer inspection, it turned out to merely be a small refrigerator.

Now would perhaps be a good time to note that, similar to how we could see a decent way through the mud and dirt underground, we could also see through more solid materials if we focused our minds on doing so. It worked a bit like focusing both of your eyes on a single point until you started seeing double. As a result of this, we were able to quickly confirm that there was nothing inside that little refrigerator without having to open the door or peek our heads inside.

After looking around for a while, Ryo and I linked back up and talked strategy.

"Doesn't make sense for both of us to be searching the same area," he said. "I'm gonna head up along the tracks facing east."

"Okay, then I'll check the west side," I said. "Oh yeah—if you see any empty lots along the road where a car could easily park, be sure to check those extra carefully. We're all but certain that the killer drove Ayane-san to the place he buried her with the same car he ran over her in."

"Roger that, chief."

We carried on searching like this for what felt like an hour, but to no avail. We agreed to check along another set of tracks that passed through a nearby residential neighborhood next. Regrettably, things got a lot more complicated underground in areas where people actually lived and worked—there were all sorts of cables, plumbing lines, and building foundations to weave through. All we could do was strain our eyes and try our best to seek out anything remotely suitcase-shaped amidst a veritable jungle of urban engineering.

"Why don't we go take a quick break in there to catch our breath?" Ayane eventually suggested after another long stretch of no leads whatsoever. She pointed to a train passing through on the tracks nearby—its golden window lights shot through the night like a line of shooting stars. We flew after it and let our incorporeal selves through the outer walls of one of the passenger cars. There was almost nobody on board, and we lined up along a row of empty seats and sat down to take a breather. Never mind that we weren't *actually* sitting, as our butts would have passed right through the seats—it was just to give the appearance of recreation. It may have seemed silly, but this alone was enough to trick our minds into relaxation mode.

"Not having too much luck so far, are we?" I said, just to fill the silence.

"Well, no. But it's only day two, remember?" said Ayane. "I'd be astounded if we somehow managed to find it this quickly."

The seats on the train were situated in such a way that we were looking directly at the windows on the opposite wall.

Normally, we would have been able to see our reflections in the glass—but in this form, all we could see was a row of empty seats. This, perhaps even more than even the flying and formlessness, drove home for me the fact that I was a ghost right now, if only temporarily.

"Do you resent your killer, Ayane-san?" asked Aoi. "Because personally, if I got killed like that, I'd go loom over their bedside every night and try to haunt the heck out of 'em until they lost their mind. You ever feel that urge?"

Ayane absolutely had the right to detest the man who killed her. It wasn't as though it was a totally avoidable accident—and she hadn't even died from the initial impact, for that matter. For instance, had he rushed her straight to the hospital, rather than act rashly out of self-preservation, she would likely still be alive today.

"I wouldn't say I've completely forgiven him," said Ayane. "But for whatever reason, I've kind of gotten over it, as weird as that sounds. I do think he deserves to be judged in the eyes of the law for covering up the accident and not coming clean to the police, but... To be completely honest, I resent myself for getting in that fight with my mom far more than I resent the driver who ran me over."

"You're awfully mature, Ayane-san," said Aoi. "Meanwhile, here I am, planning to write out the names of every one of my bullies and what they did to me in my suicide note. I want to make them suffer and live in fear as much as I possibly can after I'm gone."

"I guarantee you it won't do much to harm them in the long run," Ryo interrupted. "Maybe they'll be sorry they got busted—but it sure as hell won't make them regret what they did. Bullies like that are the type to show up at your funeral and take selfies with your open casket and then share 'em around."

"Well, how would *you* suggest I do some serious mental damage to them, then?"

"Not my wheelhouse, sorry. You'll have to figure that one out for yourself."

After resting a bit longer, we resumed our search—but it wasn't long until we hit the time limit and our souls were instantly pulled back into our bodies at the abandoned airfield. The sudden return to gravity caused Aoi to lose her balance and she fell onto her backside. Ryo scanned the area for a few moments to confirm for himself that Ayane really was nowhere to be found. And seconds later, we were all cradling our aching heads in our hands.

"Guess we'd better call it a night," I suggested, and the other two agreed. The three of us left the airfield behind and headed for home.

We met up again to continue our search the next day, and the day after that. I would go to cram school in the afternoon and then meet up with Aoi and Ryo at the station in the evening. From there, we'd go buy some sparklers, and then we'd hop on the bus and head for the abandoned airfield. On both days, I told my mother I'd be staying late at cram school to finish up what I'd been studying. There were quite a few kids who actually *did* do this, so it wasn't a significant cause for suspicion, and I knew she was too busy with her own work as of late to pay much mind to my nightly activities.

That said, I still hadn't done a single piece of artwork since the sketchbook debacle, even though I probably could have gotten away with it just by hiding my drawings in a notebook somewhere else. And if I was really worried about her finding it, I could simply find somewhere to stow it outside of the house, like in a coin locker in town or something. But I just couldn't summon forth the will to draw anymore; perhaps being forced to destroy my own artwork with my own two hands had killed my motivation completely—destroyed something vital deep inside of me. Maybe if I'd mustered up the nerve to stand up to her and protect my artwork at all costs, I could still find the urge to draw. However, I put my own self-preservation above my passion, and that was a betrayal that my inner will to create simply could not forgive. It packed up its bags and left me, maybe even for good. My mother would certainly like that, at least. It'd be her ideal outcome.

Aoi had brought up the subject of resentment the other night—and how she hoped she could do permanent mental damage to those who had bullied her and pushed her into committing suicide. I had to wonder—if I were to pick a target of my resentment, would it be my mother? She seemed to be the obvious choice, but I really didn't bear her strong enough ill will to bother leaving an even slightly passive-aggressive suicide note. In fact, at this point in time, I wasn't really planning on writing one at all. This would no doubt make all of the adults in my life try to speculate as to why I chose to take my own life. They would no doubt relish the opportunity to diagnose me somehow—be it a mental breakdown due to too much studying and the pressure of impending entrance exams, or what have you.

In reality, though, it couldn't be simpler—I just had no desire to go on living any longer. I felt distinctly disillusioned with the prospect and had given up on all my prior ambitions. And on top of that, I was a coward who couldn't even pursue the few things in life I *did* feel passionate about. I was a puppet dancing from my mother's strings. An empty vessel whose only job was to play the role of her good little honor student. That was all I was. But if I could manage this one last thing and take the reins away from her by taking my own life? I could at least prove that it had been *my* life, and *my* choice in the end.

And yes, I knew that my reason for committing suicide was pathetically minor compared to the problems Aoi and Ryo were dealing with. To say I'd simply grown tired of living was not an oversimplification—it really *did* sum it all up. I wondered how it was that the vast majority of society, people who never seriously contemplated suicide, managed to carry on living so easily. Were they simply well-off, or just happy with their lot in life? Did they all have dreams and aspirations that spurred them onward? People who went through life with distinct goals in mind always amazed me—people who never wavered in their paths, simply because they held something in their hearts to believe in. It was said that suicide rates were lower in countries with more religious populations, but I wondered if it had more to do with the act being forbidden by their respective faiths, or if simply having something greater to believe in was what got them through the day.

One night, as Ryo and I gazed down at a railroad junction during our search for the suitcase, he randomly opened up to me. He spoke about his own inner turmoil in a much more candid way than he ever had before.

"Y'know, looking back on it now, it's hard not to feel like my life didn't amount to anything at all," he said. "I mean, I was born, got to be alive for all of a split second, then disappeared just as quick, like a damn soap bubble—never leaving my mark on society or anything at all. But I figure if I can help solve the mystery of the Summer Ghost's missing body, then I can at least say I accomplished *something* before I died, you feel me? I dunno, maybe I'm just still not over having to quit the basketball team before I ever had a chance to really shine. I'm pretty jealous of those guys, to be real. They've all got futures ahead of them that are theirs for the taking. Honestly, I feel like I've been getting more and more petty and jealous toward people who get to live full, long lives lately. Like, if I was doomed to just kick the bucket before the age of twenty without leaving anything behind worth remembering, then why the hell was I even born, y'know? In the grand scheme of things, what impact did my life have on the universe, really?"

I didn't have answers that could allay any of Ryo's inner doubts and misgivings, so all I could really do was keep quiet and hear him out. I knew that acting like I understood his pain and trying to assuage his fears with pleasant-sounding but ultimately empty reassurances would only earn his contempt.

We had now scoured through more than 80 percent of the total area we originally outlined for our search, but still there was no sign of Ayane's body. It was entirely possible that we overlooked something somewhere, as we were moving through the earth rather quickly to cover as much ground as possible. The notion that we simply flew right past it without noticing and crossed that area off the list was not a pleasant one.

"I'm sorry, you guys," said Aoi. "If only I were better at flying, we could be doing this so much more efficiently."

She had indeed never really gotten the hang of flying and was still going around hand in hand with Ayane as a single unit.

"There's really no special trick to it, Aoi-chan," said Ayane. "You only have to tell your soul where you want it to go. Just calm your mind and picture your destination in your head. You can go anywhere your heart wants to."

Occasionally, Ayane would attempt to take off the training wheels like this and let go of Aoi's hand to see if she was finally ready to fly on her own. But every time, Aoi would just start spinning in midair, unable to make progress moving forward in any direction. The few times it *did* seem like she figured out how to move toward a given point, she ended up zipping off at some obscene angle in the opposite direction just moments later.

"Sorry! I guess I just suck at picking one direction and sticking with it..." said Aoi. "Maybe it's my lack of self-confidence. I just shrivel up and get cold feet, and then I can't move forward no matter what I do. Then, I start spinning in place, and eventually I lose control and go flying off like a bat out of heck in some random direction I didn't ask for."

Perhaps this was a manifestation of the same sort of escapism that led Aoi to become a shut-in truant just to get away from her bullies at school. I had no doubt that she didn't *want* to be cooped up in her room like a hermit all day.

"It's okay," Ayane reassured her. "We can just keep holding hands, then. I'll keep my eyes peeled moving forward, and you can take a closer look at things from behind as we pass them by. Just having another pair of eyes to help me find my body is all that's important to me. That alone more than doubles our chances of success."

And so we soldiered on, scouring through the underground like scuba divers investigating an old shipwreck—or like jungle expeditioners carving our way through an undergrowth of urban infrastructure—all in search of one irksomely elusive suitcase.

Whenever we stopped to take a breather, Ayane would ask us all the same question: "Why *are* you all so intent on helping me find my body anyway?"

Why indeed. At first, it had certainly been for her sake—I wanted to unearth her buried remains and give her soul a chance to finally breathe again. But now? I wasn't so sure anymore. Maybe we were all just trying to grow more acquainted with death in our own ways, so we'd be ready for it ourselves when the time came. Perhaps the corpse we'd find upon opening that suitcase would be not just Ayane's, but the final nail in each of our own coffins as well—a representation of death we couldn't deny.

The four of us flew through the night sky.

The city lights burned bright beneath us. In every lit window of every home was a living person—or a family.

It was almost too much to take in, trying to imagine them all at once.

And then, before we knew it, it was upon us—the last night of summer vacation.

Granted, it wasn't as if the end of August marked the end of summer itself—it simply meant it was the start of the second semester at school. If we weren't able to find the suitcase tonight, we could still keep coming back and looking for it until autumn truly came, or so I tried to tell myself. But I knew that being back in the swing of things academically would limit our availability quite a bit—even if Aoi still wasn't planning on going back to school, apparently.

"It's not that I don't try," she said. "I still put on my uniform in the morning and *try* going to school sometimes. Heck, I even *want* to go there and learn. But as soon as I walk up to campus, I just get so nauseous that I want to puke. I'll curl up in a little ball on the roadside, and I literally can't move a muscle until I wait it out."

Her parents also didn't seem to have any intention of forcing her to go.

"Oh yeah, no. My folks couldn't care less," she explained. "My dad just thinks of me as some baggage he was forced to bring along from his first marriage. There's no emotional or blood connection between me and my stepmom either."

We'd decided to spend that night searching along a stretch of railroad that ran from the edge of the city's residential area right up to the prefectural border. We skimmed along the tracks as they shined beneath the cool moonlight, dodging the occasional train carrying tired salarymen home from work as we dipped down beneath the earth in search of our quarry. After an hour or so of searching failed to turn up anything, we moved on to the next location and picked up from there.

"Any luck?" asked Ryo as he passed me by at one point.

"Nope," I said.

"Man… If it's not here, then where the hell else do we look?"

"We might have to loosen our criteria for where to search a bit," I said. "Either that or we overlooked it somehow, and we'll have to slowly retrace our steps through everywhere we've checked previously."

Just then, I heard Ayane calling out to us.

"Tomoya-kun! Ryo-kun! Where are you two?"

Her voice was coming from up above. Ryo and I lifted our heads to look up at her, floating high above the train tracks. Her usual hand-holding partner was notably not along for the ride this time.

"What's up?" I asked.

"I can't find Aoi-chan," she said, her tone somewhat frantic. "We were trying to practice letting her fly on her own again, so we went searching through the ground without holding hands. At first, she seemed to be doing just fine, but I took my eyes off of her for one second, and I guess she must've whooshed off somewhere..."

Oh, great. There was no predicting Aoi's movements once she lost control like that—she'd go bounding around at light speed at sharp angles that totally defied the laws of inertia (which the rest of our minds generally adhered to, despite it not being strictly required). Finding her would not be an easy task.

"Maybe we should just leave her be?" I suggested.

"Yeah, I mean, she'll still wake up back in her body at the end of the night, right?" Ryo offered in agreement.

"Wow, you two are pretty heartless," said Ayane.

"Fine. Where did you last see her?" I asked.

"Back over there." She pointed down along the tracks.

"Okay... Why don't we head over in that direction then? We can still continue the search while keeping an eye out for her underground."

I wondered just how far it was possible to fly while in ghost form—assuming there were any limits at all. Could you fly through the stratosphere and out among the solar system? Could you delve deeper into the Earth's core than mankind had ever done before? I was mildly curious, but oddly not so much that I would ever bother trying to do so myself. And for whatever reason, something told me we wouldn't be able to go too far beyond the sphere in which our daily lives took place, even if we tried. It was almost like instinctive knowledge; perhaps all wandering spirits were bound to a central location. In that case, my suggestion to Ayane a while back about her still being able to go out and see the world may not have been a viable option after all.

Such were my absentminded thoughts as we flew around looking for both the suitcase and Aoi—until eventually, I caught a glimpse of a hazy silhouette that looked vaguely similar to the latter, floating awkwardly off in the distance.

"Hey guys!" she cried out, waving her hands back and forth as she fumbled her way toward us through the air. "You guys, come quick! I think I might have found the suitcase!"

Upon regrouping with us, Aoi explained that this discovery had apparently been a total coincidence. She was flying alongside Ayane when she got careless for a moment and lost her sense of balance. Then, upon attempting to set herself upright again, she got suddenly and completely turned around before wildly spinning out as she went barreling off in a completely random direction. From the way she described it, it sounded almost like she'd been dipping in and out of the underground at peak velocity like a broken rocket on a wonky trajectory, struggling to break out of Earth's orbit. And try as she might, there was nothing she could do to stop herself, apparently.

"It really felt like I was clinging for dear life to a bucking bronco or something!" she exclaimed. "Honestly, I thought I was gonna die for a minute there."

She then recounted how, eventually, she broke out of this cycle and shot high up into the sky and cut a sharp curve over the city, like a shooting star. After passing over countless apartment buildings and residential homes, she eventually fell back down to earth—diving through everything from a dining room where a family was just sitting down to eat dinner, to an older couple's living room as the pair watched TV, to a convenience store where a lone employee was dutifully restocking shelves. When she at last regained control over her altitude, she found herself hovering in the air near a large radio tower—but was still unable to stop spinning rapidly in circles. She shut her eyes tight in an attempt to stave off the dizziness from her whirling vision, and it was then that she remembered what Ayane had told her—about how she could go anywhere her heart desired if she could only picture it in her mind.

Where do *I want to go?* she thought, and all of a sudden, she stopped spinning in midair. Her body went completely still. Finally able to catch her breath, she calmed down and tried her damnedest to head back in the direction from which she came. She knew that if could just make her way to the railroad and follow it underground, she'd be able to meet back up with us eventually. Noticing a set of tracks that conveniently ran right alongside the radio tower, she dived down into the murky, fathomless underground.

"But then I couldn't pick which way to go down the tracks," said Aoi. "I had completely lost my bearings and had no idea which one would lead me back to you guys. So I just kind of hung out there for a sec, not sure what to do...and that's when I saw it, right there in front of me."

There in the ground, not even a meter below the surface, was something. It was a large, rectangular, boxlike object—just large enough for a human to fit inside.

We all followed Aoi back to the site of this discovery—an empty lot surrounded by a chain-link fence on the outskirts of town. A lone radio tower stood above it with little white flowers clustered around its feet. And sure enough, it was there that we found the object Aoi had described—a suitcase, large enough to be taken on a several-week-long overseas trip.

We all simply looked up at it in silence from where we were submerged, slightly below it in the ground.

I strained my eyes, and the outer shell of the luggage became slightly transparent, allowing me a vague glimpse of what was inside. Even though it was already hard enough to see anything underground through the mud and earth, I could see the pale moonlight shining down from high above the surface—illuminating the suitcase and its contents from behind.

"This is it," said Ayane. "That's me."

Her voice was filled with a soft sort of reverence as she stared up at the suitcase and the silhouette of the curled-up human form that had been laid to rest therein.

And that was the last thing I saw before my vision blacked out.

Our time had run out, apparently—and the three of us were forcibly snapped back into our bodies where we left them at the abandoned airfield. The sparkler I was holding hours prior fizzled out and fell from my fingers down onto the runway. As the sudden headache hit my brain, I looked around. Ayane was nowhere to be seen.

"You guys remember where that place was?" asked Ryo.

"More or less, yeah..." Aoi mumbled.

"Hell yeah! Now *that's* what I'm talkin' about! Way to go, Aoi!" cheered Ryo.

"Wait, what?" she asked. "What did *I* do? Are you being sarcastic?"

"Hell no, dude! You found the suitcase! All by yourself!"

The two of them then turned to me as if waiting for some sort of signal.

"Let's go check it out," I said, and the two of them nodded.

We left the abandoned airfield and set off in that direction using the GPS maps on our phones to determine where exactly we had just been. It was about an hour's walk from where we currently stood—across the floodplain, down along the edge of the prefecture, and through some residential neighborhoods. We stopped just once at a convenience store along the way to take a short breather and buy some bottled beverages.

"I wonder what's gonna happen to Ayane-san once we unearth her body," Aoi said as we walked. "You think that'll give her inner peace so her soul can finally move on, and we'll never see her again?"

"Hard to say," I replied. "She told me she doesn't believe in an afterlife, though."

For religious people, the notion of one's soul "moving on" to the next life generally implied entering into the Kingdom of Heaven, or Sukhavati, or whatever equivalent that person believed in. But even assuming some such paradise existed—which I was doubtful of—would it even be possible for a non-believer to enter?

I noticed Ryo was lagging pretty far behind us. He didn't seem to have the same level of stamina as the two of us, judging by his shortness of breath.

"You okay, Ryo-kun?" Aoi asked, jogging over to his side.

"Man, I'm such a loser..." he muttered, his voice and expression both full of chagrin. "Gettin' all bushed from a little walk like this... You two go on ahead. I'll catch up."

"No way, buster," said Aoi. She then turned to address me. "I'll hang back here with him. You keep going, Tomoya-kun."

I nodded. "Okay."

I left the two of them behind and hurried on toward my destination. It wasn't long before I reached the area we were exploring earlier. A passenger train with its windows aglow loudly passed through down the tracks that stretched through the suburban streets. I followed them all the way to the edge of the neighborhood, where the buildings got sparser and there was more untouched nature than developed land. In a thicket up ahead, I could see the silhouette of the radio tower, jutting defiantly upward into the starry sky overhead. The suitcase was buried beneath its feet. I was close now, I realized—and so I broke into a sprint.

The lot containing the radio tower was situated right up against the tracks and enclosed by a chain-link fence nearly three meters high. The only feasible way in seemed to be by climbing up and over. I slowly made my way up, using the gaps in the fence as makeshift footholds. There was apparently a sharp portion of wire at the top of the fence and when I gripped it to pull myself over, it tore open my palms—but I was too focused on my objective at that moment to pay the pain any mind. I hoisted myself over and jumped down inside the property.

The suitcase had been buried directly beneath a small bed of white flowers at the tower's feet, so it didn't take long to find the right spot. However, it was only then that I realized that I neglected to bring along digging implements of any description. Having no other choice, I grabbed a piece of scrap lumber lying on the ground nearby and started shoveling away—stabbing it into the ground until the soil was soft enough to scrape out. It was slow going, but eventually the hole started getting bigger and bigger.

As I plowed away at it, bits of mud splattered up onto my face and sweat started trickling down my cheeks. I took a short break when I felt my phone buzzing. I looked to see who was calling me, but it was only my mother. Presumably, she was confused about getting home from work late only to discover that I was nowhere to be found and was now calling to ask my whereabouts. I turned my phone off and got back to digging.

Eventually, I heard someone calling my name. I looked over my shoulder and saw that Ryo and Aoi were now standing on the other side of the chain-link fence. Neither of them seemed to have enough energy left to climb over it and help me dig, so all they could do was watch as I drove the plank repeatedly into the hole and scooped out clump after clump of dirt. After a while of this, my arm muscles started to burn, and all I could hear were the sounds of earth being displaced and my own labored breathing. The exhaustion built up faster than I expected, and I started getting so lightheaded that I was honestly worried I might pass out.

A train ran right by the lot—its window lights briefly piercing the darkness as it rumbled thunderously through the woods. And then, it happened—my makeshift shovel struck against something, and I felt the reverberations course through my arms. I scraped away the surrounding dirt, and finally unearthed the silver lid of the suitcase.

Seeing me stop dead in my tracks, Ryo and Aoi called out from behind me—but I was too exhausted to even make out their words. I could only assume they were asking if I found it. I wiped the sweat from my eyes with my mud-caked forearm. I brushed away the last of the dirt on the suitcase lid—there were a few scratches on its surface, but it was in extremely good condition overall, and was definitely large enough to fit a person inside. I felt around for the metal fixtures to unlatch it, and although there was a bit of resistance, my efforts were eventually rewarded with a satisfying click. There didn't seem to be any other locks or anything on the suitcase itself, so I lifted the lid and opened it up.

I could feel Ryo and Aoi watching with bated breath behind me.

I gazed down at Ayane, curled up inside the suitcase.

"Phew! That's better."

She sat up, stretched out her arms, and took a deep breath of the crisp night air. After filling her lungs, Ayane turned to me with a warm, satisfied smile on her face.

"Thanks, Tomoya-kun," she said. "This means a lot."

But that was just a hallucination.

The Ayane that was curled up in front of me was only a lifeless corpse.

Six

Summer Ghost

When I walked in the front door late that night and my mother saw me covered from head to toe in mud, she seemed rather taken aback. When she asked what happened, I spun a convoluted lie about getting jumped by a group of delinquents on my way home from cram school. She could tell from my exhausted expression that I had at least not been out having unauthorized fun around town all night, so she reluctantly bought my story. I took a quick shower and went straight to bed.

Morning came swiftly.

It was September 1st—one of the most popular days for suicides among minors. With every muscle in my body still sore from the previous night, I trudged my way over to school for the first day of the second semester. I walked into the classroom and was greeted by the familiar indifference of my fellow classmates. Then in came my homeroom teacher, and first period began shortly thereafter.

Summer vacation was officially over.

"Hey, like, did you guys hear about this?"

During passing period, one of the girls in my class recounted an interesting anecdote to a few other female classmates gathered around her desk.

"Apparently, they found a *dead body* in my neighborhood!" she said—and I perked up my ears to listen (while still pretending to be sleeping with my head down). "No joke! When I woke up this morning, the whole street was *full* of police cars. I guess they got an anonymous tip overnight or something. Everyone was just standing outside in their pajamas, trying to figure out who it might be and what exactly happened."

Apparently, this girl's mother heard a rumor through the neighborhood grapevine that a body was found in a suitcase in a fenced-off lot near the railroad. I was relieved to hear that the police did their job and followed through on the report in a prompt manner and didn't dismiss it as a prank or anything like that. The three of us had called it in last night, of course—but we made ourselves scarce before the police could actually show up on the scene. I even made sure to wipe down the suitcase with a handkerchief, so I didn't leave any of my own fingerprints.

By the time I got home from school that day, the discovery was already being covered on national news. A few days later, they reported that they managed to discern the victim's identity, and they started showing Ayane's name and photo on TV alongside the police's official theory that she got herself mixed up in some sort of major incident or scandal by accident. It wasn't long after that that a man came forth and turned himself in to the authorities, claiming to be the owner of the suitcase and admitting that he accidentally hit Ayane with his car on the night of a typhoon, three years prior. He had apparently been racked by extreme guilt ever since, and the recent flood of news reports led him to decide he couldn't run from his crime any longer. He admitted everything to the police—it was an open-and-shut case. The only detail that remained mysteriously unknown was the identity of the anonymous caller who dug up the body in its very specific, very difficult to access burial location.

Ryo, Aoi, and I stayed in touch via our group DM, sharing opinions with one another anytime new information came to light regarding the incident. Then, about halfway through September, we all got together on the weekend and headed back to the abandoned airfield at nightfall with sparklers in hand. We wanted to test to see if we could still meet with Ayane or not. The last time any of us had spoken with her was the night we discovered the suitcase under the ground. But now, no matter how many sparklers we burned through, she wouldn't appear before us. The three of us couldn't come to a consensus as to whether it was simply because summer was already over or because finding her body allowed her soul to finally rest in peace.

But I did see her one last time after that—while I was sleeping.

In my dream, she and I were taking a walk together through what appeared to be an amusement park. It was clearly not anywhere in the real world, however, as all of the buildings and attractions were oddly colorless—almost like a blank canvas version of an amusement park, still waiting to receive its hues. A pure white merry-go-round, a pure white roller coaster—the flowers and ornamental vegetation were all pure white as well. Ayane was not floating, notably, but walking on her own two feet beside me. The park was completely deserted as well, with no other guests in sight aside from us two.

"But tell me, though," Ayane said as we walked down the path. "What is it you *really* want to do?"

The context in which this question was being asked of me was entirely unclear. But context was often hazy at best in a dream, so perhaps that was to be expected.

"Guess I wouldn't mind going for a ride on that thing," I answered, pointing to a large Ferris wheel across the way. Its spokes and carriages were all the same shade of pure, unblemished white.

"I really wanted to live, you know," she said. "Maybe that's why I feel so strongly about wanting the same for you."

She stopped dead in her tracks and looked me straight in the eye. Her facial features were as striking and as flawless as ever.

"Besides," she went on, "you can only draw while you're still alive. You can't very well pick up a pencil once you're dead, now can you?"

I was suddenly reminded of the fact that I hadn't drawn anything in months. I wondered if that part of me was already dead, or if there was still a spark of that desire somewhere deep down inside me, just waiting to be rekindled.

Ayane turned and started trotting off down the path once again.

"You...want me to live, Ayane-san?" I asked, jogging to catch up with her.

"Of course I do," she said.

"But why?"

"Because I've kind of got a thing for older guys."

That was decidedly not among the possible answers I was expecting.

"I mean, think about it, Tomoya-kun. If you were to die right now, then you'd be younger than me for all eternity. And to be completely honest with you, I'd *never* consider dating a guy who was still in high school. So, if you really insist on dying, at least do me a favor and wait a little longer—until you're a bit older than me, y'know? Trust me—I'm just trying to help us both out here. You just go ahead and grow up into a handsome old silver fox and *then* you can come over here and be with me. Sound good?"

"...I'm starting to have second thoughts about my taste in women," I mumbled.

"Oh, come on—I'm just messing with you. Though I really *do* want you to go on living. And I really *do* have a thing for older guys."

She then took me by the hand. Her fingers were ice cold, but her touch felt oddly warm.

"I'm really grateful to you, you know," she said. "If you hadn't come along and found my body, I might've never made it back home to my mom. I wish nothing but the best for you in life, Tomoya-kun. I don't know if there's a god out there, so I don't know to who I could possibly pray to make it come true. But just know that there's one dead girl out there who'll always be thinking about you, and who genuinely hopes you'll have the most incredible life imaginable. So don't forget that. I'll see you around, Tomoya-kun—bye now."

As soon as she said those words, my eyes shot wide open, and I was left staring up at my bedroom ceiling—basking in the afterglow of a dream I wished I could have savored just a little bit longer.

As winter came around the bend, Ryo's health really began to deteriorate. The disease was rapidly taking over more and more of his body. And it was just as this progression seemed to be taking a turn for the worse that I got a rather unexpected update—he and Aoi had officially become an item.

I had no idea they were even somewhat romantically interested, so it came as a pretty big shock to me. However, I didn't take it personally; apparently, they privately stayed in touch and got to know each other pretty well over the fall. I sent them a quick message of congratulations, and almost immediately received a photo in reply: a selfie of the two of them sitting next to each other in Ryo's hospital bed. He looked awfully emaciated.

December 24th—after finishing my studies at cram school, I headed not for home, but for a tall department store building near the station. The pedestrians passing me by on the sidewalk were all bundled up in thick coats and scarves. Christmas music played all throughout downtown, and colorful lights adorned the trees lining the road. The windows of a street-level café were decorated with Santas and crucifixes—the latter of which reminded me of my father and his beloved rosary.

I had scoped out the building beforehand, so I knew that anyone could easily reach the rooftop just by taking the elevator all the way up. As I peered down over the edge onto the streets below, I was reminded once again just how tall this particular building was—the chances of surviving a fall from this height were miniscule indeed. There were also very few pedestrians walking by on this side of the building, so the chances of accidentally hitting an innocent bystander were slim to none. Sure, there was a small fence around the perimeter of the roof, but it was nothing I couldn't hop over. Basically, all there was left to do would be to actually take the plunge.

The cold wind brushed against my cheeks. I set my heavy backpack, full of reference texts and practice workbooks, down at my feet. I gripped the railing with my fingers and gazed down at the city below. Being so close to the station, the buildings around here were densely packed together. I couldn't hear any of the Christmas music I heard down on the streets a few minutes ago—only the howling of the wind.

My original intent was to end it all before the year was over, but I just couldn't get the conversation I'd had with Ayane in my dreams that night out of my head.

"I really wanted to live, you know. Maybe that's why I feel so strongly about wanting the same for you."

I knew it had only been a dream, and that it wasn't the real Ayane who'd said this to me—just a figment of my imagination. But even so, I assumed my subconscious showed me that dream for a reason. Perhaps it was because somewhere deep down, I really *did* want to go on living, and so my brain conjured that facsimile of her to beg me not to end it all—using *her* face, and *her* voice. Either that, or it really *was* a message from the real Ayane, who came back to visit me from beyond the grave to thank me for all that I'd done for her.

I hoped that by the time I was out here on the rooftop I'd know for certain whether or not I still wanted to die, or if that urge had left me. But even now that I stood here, I couldn't say for sure.

Perhaps I should jump the fence and lean out over the edge? Maybe putting myself one step, one false move away from letting it all go could force some honesty out of me. Perhaps I might even do it too—let go, right there and then.

And yet the moment I gripped the railing to jump over it, it started to snow. The world was gently bathed in a whirlwind of white, powdery specks that danced through the air like tiny feathers. I gazed up into the night sky and watched them fall down over me, and the entire city, from the billowing clouds up above.

"I wish nothing but the best for you in life, Tomoya-kun."

For whatever reason, what popped into my mind was her expression—the look she gave me as she said those very words. I ruminated over the full depth of their sentiment, and a strange warmth filled my chest. With it came a familiar pang of longing—one I knew all too well. It was the irrepressible urge to sketch this image down on paper as soon as possible, lest it vanish from my mind forever. I wanted to leave this mark, this final impression of her on the world forever.

And so I didn't end up jumping from the rooftop that day. Instead, on my way back home, I stopped by the little art supply store I used to visit back in middle school and bought myself a crisp new sketchbook—one just brimming with possibilities.

"Sooo... You dead yet?" Aoi asked me via DM over the New Year holiday. Apparently, she remembered what I told the two of them before about my ideal suicide timeframe.

"Nope. Not yet," I wrote back—even though it was pretty redundant to type, as I wouldn't be able to respond to begin with if I were. Then, after a moment's hesitation, I added, *"I think I'd like to try seeing what actually being alive feels like for a while."*

Seven

Summer Ghost

THE SPARKLER BEGAN TO GLOW as I lit the few grains of gunpowder embedded in its tissue-paper tip. Only a few seconds later, this initial spark swelled up into a slag—a molten dewdrop dangling delicately from the end of the crooked stick; a mote of warmth, carved out from the cold. Suspended upside down, this orb of light burned most brightly from the bottom, as the resultant updraft from the tiny pocket of heat it created only drew in more and more oxygen to fuel its flame. And so on it burned in the crisp night air, bright and brittle until at last it saw fit to begin shedding sparks, and a firework was born at last.

For a moment, the crackling embers scattered wildly—each firing off in their own arcs before bursting and branching out in all directions—but then, all at once, the fizzling fountain froze over. The chirping insects in the surrounding fields and forests fell silent, and the flow of time seemed to slow to a crawl. This was a sensation I hadn't felt in over a year—a strange phenomenon that could only be experienced here in this spot where the fabric of our world grew thin, and the fetters that kept us bound to it came undone.

Aoi was standing right beside me.

And directly across from us was Ryo.

The three of us stood huddled close together in a triangle, as if gathered to marvel at the sparks where they hung frozen in midair.

"Been a long time since we all got together like this," said Aoi.

"Yeah, no kidding," I said with a nod. "I've been so busy lately that I couldn't afford to make the trip back home. Sorry you two had to wait up for me."

"Don't sweat it, dude. Just glad you could make it," Ryo said, casting his gaze up into the sky. "Man, it's hard to believe it's been a whole year though, huh?"

Far off in the distance, the skies overhead had begun to fade from black into a deep, navy blue. It was that most fragile time of night, just before the first rays of morning light crept up over the horizon, and for a moment, I could almost see her there with us—that pale, fleeting specter I once knew. But as of yet, there were no reports online of anyone having encountered her this summer.

"Guess Ayane-san's not coming," Aoi said. "Too bad."

She was right. Based on our experiences last summer, Ayane should have already appeared by now. But tonight, she was nowhere to be found.

"Yeah, I think she… I think she finally managed to find closure," I said. "And now her soul's moved on to wherever it was going next."

Where exactly that might be, none of us could say, but we should wish her well all the same. Yes, we would never see her again, and yes, even the urban legend of the Summer Ghost would likely fade into obscurity before long. But I knew I'd still remember her and think of her fondly each year, whenever summer came.

Ryo called out to me. "Hey, Tomoya. How've you been doin' lately? Still hangin' in there?"

"I'm doing all right, yeah," I said. "Just working and studying so I can retake my entrance exams and hopefully get into art school next year. I finally managed to move out and get my own place too. That's the main reason I haven't been able to come back until now, actually—I've just been so busy with the move and my new job and everything."

When I thought back on all that had happened over the past six months, I couldn't help but get a bit emotional. Despite making the decision to put suicide on hold and give living a good college try for a while, I did not initially feel at all motivated to give college a try. When the day of the entrance exam for what had been my first-choice university finally rolled around, I didn't even show up to the testing site. Instead, I went for a long walk with my sketchbook along the shoreline, stopping every now and then to sit down and draw any particularly beautiful bits of scenery I encountered.

I wasn't sure who exactly might have noticed my absence—maybe one of my studying acquaintances realized I was missing and let the officiators know—but before I knew it, I was getting calls and texts from all sorts of people. My mother, my homeroom teacher, my cram school instructor... all of them disgruntled, distressed, and in disbelief. They all seemed to agree that I just threw my life away. Maybe I had. I applied to a number of universities and paid the preliminary examination fees for them all, but I didn't show up to take a single test. The once-supportive adults in my life wasted no time in branding me a living failure.

And so I set forth on a crash course for graduation with no higher education or employment plan whatsoever. As word of my life choices spread throughout the school, I could feel the judgmental glances of my peers whenever I walked down the hallway. Apparently, the leading theory was that I cracked under the pressure of all the studying and expectations of me as an honor student and had something of a mental breakdown. But to be quite honest, I didn't really care what people thought about me, though.

In the past, I was very careful not to be defiant or rebellious toward my mother and her wishes. It was something of a self-preservation tactic that allowed the two of us to go on living together in harmony. So, I wondered what exactly it was that had convinced me to drop the act and stop being so obsessed with maintaining the status quo. Perhaps my respect for her absolute authority as my parent was beginning to fade now that I was quickly approaching adulthood myself. Or perhaps my desire to express myself through artwork finally tipped the scales and overruled my fear of anything she could possibly do to me. But whatever the reason, I decided that now I was going to hold fast to this passion I held within my chest. I wouldn't let anyone's sharp words or derisive laughter dissuade me from pursuing this most vital urge, this compulsion to create, ever again.

After graduating from high school, I made the decision—and this time of my own volition—to start attending a preparatory cram school for those interested in applying to a university of the arts. My mother and I fought vehemently over it. Despite her claims to the contrary, I hadn't lost all love and respect for her as a parent. I was deeply grateful for her constant efforts to support our little family as a single parent, often working late into the night just to make ends meet. I also did not think this decision on my part should constitute a unilateral severing of our familial ties.

"I brought you into this world, so it falls to me to make sure you find and stick to the right track through life."

There was still a part of me that did respect her in the way she insisted—as my "creator," in a sense—so I did still feel a deep-seated aversion to deliberately going against her wishes. But now that I found my own footing, I could finally see my mother for what she truly was: an equal, no more or less valid than me. Having done that, I could rationalize that there was no need for me to feel indebted to her to the point of self-erasure.

"Though I do sometimes feel like maybe I had it easier back when I was just trying to play the role of honor student," I admitted to my friends aloud.

Try as I did to reason with my mother, I eventually grew tired of her incessant attempts to mentally break me down with cutting words and sneers whenever I discussed my life goals. But thankfully, I no longer had to deal with her much now that I'd moved out on my own. My life had grown far more peaceful ever since.

Interestingly, it seemed my father somehow heard that I was now living by myself, and one afternoon, I received a postcard from him in the mail. My constant fighting with my mother over my "poor life decisions" had become a somewhat frequent subject of neighborhood gossip, apparently, so perhaps one of the Christian households in our area who still kept in contact with my father had keyed him in. The postcard bore an illustration of Jesus Christ being held in the arms of angels, all ascending together into the sky. On the back, he wrote a short message expressing his support for my new choice of lifestyle. Ever since he left my mom and me, I always wondered where exactly my father was currently living. It felt a bit surreal to have his return address written so simply on that little postcard now. Maybe one day, after I got more used to living on my own, it might be nice to go and visit him.

"I think I can safely say that I haven't felt any desire to die in quite a while now," I continued. "Anytime life gets me down, I just think about how once I'm dead, I'll never be able to draw anything ever again, and that alone is enough to keep me going. As long as there's still art left in me, I'm not gonna let it die."

"I'm really glad to hear that, dude," Ryo said with a nod before turning his head. "And what about you, Aoi? Take it you've decided to go on living too?"

"Yeah," she said. "I mean, that's what you told me you wanted me to do, right? The last time we met..."

"Oh, so you *did* get that, huh? Gotta admit, I was a little worried whether my words were even getting through to you at that point. Couldn't even make sounds anymore at the end there, so I figured maybe you were just nodding along to be polite, ha ha..."

"No, no. I could read your lip movements just fine..." she replied. "Don't worry."

The last time the two of them saw each other was in Ryo's hospital room. I hadn't been there myself, but according to Aoi, Ryo was so emaciated and woozy from all of the drugs at that point that it already seemed like he was barely there, mentally. He passed away about twelve hours after she walked out the door.

A hundred tiny beads of light hung in the air around the sparkler's glowing tip. I'd long since let go of the sparkler itself, but in this time-frozen state, it remained suspended in midair as if it was weightless. The contours of Ryo's silhouette were hazy and indistinct now—just like how the Summer Ghost had been when we first met her, one year prior. Although it seemed like he was standing right here in front of us, he looked more like a mirage than a tangible being—a projection being beamed in from somewhere far away.

"I think that was my only real regret, y'know," said Ryo. "Whether or not my last words made it through to you all right."

"And *that*'s why you're still a wandering ghost right now?" she balked.

"I mean, c'mon," he countered. "Knowing you, it wouldn't be *that* crazy to assume you'd totally misheard me, would it?"

"Yes it would! How little faith in me do you have?!" Aoi pouted, puffing out her cheeks in protest.

"Anyway, it's a real load off my mind to see that you're doin' okay. Think I can finally rest easy now and move on to wherever I'm going next."

"And where do you think that might be?" I asked, curious. "The afterlife? A heaven of some sort? Does such a place actually exist?"

"Couldn't tell ya, my man," Ryo replied.

"Okay, well... Could you tell me why you didn't end up killing yourself, at least?"

Surely he was still at least partially in control of his body after being hospitalized for the last time. He could have hung himself in his bed, or perhaps gotten help from one of us to do it another way. But he didn't—and I always wondered why. I meant to ask even before he passed, actually, but as the disease progressed and his symptoms got worse and worse, I just felt like it would've been pretty tasteless to ask why he didn't take the easier route in hindsight.

Ryo just kind of looked at me for a moment. His lips curled up into a wry smirk. "It's 'cause of what you said in that message of yours—that you were gonna try seeing what actually being alive felt like for a while. I think that's what convinced me to stick things out until the very end."

"I'm...not sure I see the logical connection there."

"I mean, it would've looked pretty lame for *me* to go and off myself after *you* just had this whole cool soul-searching moment and found renewed hope in life, y'know what I mean?" he said. "Even if I still went and died like a loser in the end."

"I think it would have been pretty understandable in your situation, but okay."

"You're not a loser at all, Ryo-kun..." said Aoi. She was trying to keep calm, but she ultimately failed to hold back the tears now streaming down her cheeks. "You were really cool too, right up until the very end... Hey, you wanna know something? I'm actually going back to school now. Even though every day, the mere thought makes me so nauseous I could puke. Even though every day, just being there makes me wish I were dead. The way everyone laughs at me, and how I just can't stop making stupid mistakes... I hate every minute of it. It makes me want to run off and crawl into a ditch and die. But every time I feel that way, I think of you, Ryo-kun. And how you stayed with us and kept fighting until the very end, even though you knew the odds were stacked against you. That's what gives me the strength to get back up again. That's what makes me feel like maybe I *can* go on living after all. I can't thank you enough for that, Ryo-kun. I'm really glad I got the chance to know you, if only for a little while."

Ryo brought his hands up and stroked his thumbs across Aoi's cheeks as if to wipe her tears away—even though the streams just passed right through his fingertips. But even though he could no longer offer her any physical comfort or consolation, he still flashed her the warmest, most reassuring smile I had ever seen.

"Man, I wish I could stay and talk with you guys a whole lot longer. If only I could pull your souls out of your bodies like Ayane used to, yeah? The three of us could chill and chat here for hours."

"Why don't you give it a try?" I asked.

"Just did, when I touched Aoi's cheek. It didn't work," he said—and then turned and tried to grab me by the arm. His fingers passed right through it. "See? I can't touch you either."

"Huh. I wonder why. Maybe there's a trick to it you just don't know yet?" I thought aloud.

"Tomoya, my man... I thought you were smarter than this," said Ryo, shaking his head. "You guys can't enter ghost form 'cause your souls aren't ready to die anymore. You want to live now. Your souls don't *want* to let go of your bodies, so I can't pull them out of you. Or, well...I'm *pretty* sure that's why, anyway."

The frozen sparks that hung in midair around the sparkler's tip slowly began moving once more, tracing trails of golden light through the air. The flow of time was rapidly returning to normal.

"Looks like this is farewell, then," I said.

Aoi wiped away her tears and did her best to see Ryo off with a smile. "Goodbye, Ryo-kun," she said. "I'm glad I got to see you one last time."

"Me too, Aoi," said Ryo. "I'm glad we could talk again like this. And you too, Tomoya—thanks for showing up, man."

The eastern sky was growing brighter by the second now as the dark of night swiftly receded before the light of morning. And as it gave way, so did Ryo's spectral form begin to fade.

"See ya," he said, waving us both a casual goodbye.

As the morning sun peeked over the horizon and bathed the runway in its light, the skies overhead recalled their summer blue. Ryo's last remaining contours passed forever into memory, melting softly into the humid air. Aoi and I just stood there for a time, watching the sun rise over the asphalt where he was standing moments prior. As the wind picked up and brushed its way over the airfield, the rhythmic swaying of the tall grass all around us almost sounded like waves gently crashing against the shore.

I placed one hand on Aoi's back, and the two of us agreed that it was best we left. We snuck back out through the gap in the chain-link fence and began our homeward journey into town—but as we reached the crest of the hill overlooking the abandoned airfield, I turned back one last time and said a silent farewell to the ghost of Sato Ayane.

And with that, we headed off—each and all of us to wherever it was we were going next.

about the author

Otsuichi

Won the 6th Annual JUMP Novel Grand Prix at the age of 17 for his 1996 debut novel, *Summer, Fireworks, and My Corpse*, along with the 3rd Annual Honkaku Mystery Award for his 2002 novel *GOTH*. Other notable works include *ZOO*, *Calling You*, and the *Arknoah* series. Has written novels and short stories under several pseudonyms over the years, but now writes and directs films under his real name, Hirotaka Adachi.

about the artist

loundraw

Made his debut as an illustrator in his teens and is responsible for the cover art of such iconic novels as *I Want to Eat Your Pancreas* and *You Shine in the Moonlight*. A versatile creative who has dipped his toes in such diverse mediums as animation, fiction, manga, and songwriting. In January 2019, he established his own animation studio, FLAT STUDIO, where he directed his first theatrical feature film, *Summer Ghost*.